Dear _____

I've _____ *you this book because* _____

_____

_____

_____

_____

_____

_____

It is my hope that you will _____

_____

_____

_____

_____

_____

Moreover, I think the story on page _____

will _____

_____

_____

_____

_____

Enjoy!

Sincerely,

_____

TONY LEHOVEN'S

BRAIN FOOD

· ·

FOR THE STARVED MIND

This book is dedicated
to
You

ACKNOWLEDGEMENTS

The author would like to thank the following
for their invaluable work "under the hood".

- **Warren Dastrup**
Wingman and laugh instigator
- **Dinah LeHoven**
Editor and fact advocate
- **Elizabeth Rosner**
Final editor and word replacement engineer
- **R. Eve Solomon**
Copy proofer and ellipsis wrangler

And also Sj LeHoven as first listener, especially since I was three cups
of coffee ahead of her most of the time, Char Dyer, for her encourage-
ment and support, Jo Evans, who gave ear to my stories when I used
to write the titles first, Steven Ruddell, an awareness technician who
disrobed my stories and showed me their spiritual essence, Melinda
Morey, my bodysurfing buddy who wishes Lappert's would sell bran
muffins again, guitarist Peter Sprague for his delicious arrangements
of Beatles tunes, and my reading crew who kept me going with their
welcome commentary.

COVER ILLUSTRATION
by John S. Pritchett
email • john@pritchettcartoons.com
website • www.pritchettcartoons.com

Book design & layout
Tony LeHoven

PREFACE

Editors note: On the final day of book layout, the preface took a long look at the stories behind it, got cold feet and hid in back of the epilogue on page 172.

CONTACT

email • tony@brainfoodthebook.com
website • www.brainfoodthebook.com

CONTENTS

CONTENTS

CHAPTER THREE

CHAPTER FOUR

CHAPTER ONE

"Don't believe everything you read about mythology"
- Thor

THE JOB INTERVIEW

Fred's eyes were lamenting the invention of the computer as they stared droopily at the electronic screen. "Flash Fiction Writer Wanted" were the only words Fred could easily make out as he glassily eyed the fine print. Doubling down, Fred squinted mightily at the screen as the tiny text unblurred itself into words, then lines of information, and finally into coherent sentences. Fred perused the paragraphs and liked the gist of them.

According to the advertisement on the screen, a start-up flash fiction magazine called "Short Shorts" was looking for an editor/writer to write really short stories, 500 words or less, and to manage the magazine for a monthly salary of $1,000, no benefits included. Fred, who had never really been acquainted with a significant amount of currency, welcomed the prospect of 1,000 clams in his pocket every month. He squinted at the ad again.

Fred was a dichard old-school writer. His perpetually ink-stained hand was thin and bony, its middle finger knurled with a callus from the constant wear of the pen. He liked to write long form novels, big flowing epics with salient metaphors and adventurous digressions. Fred was excited about the prospect of writing in this new genre of flash fiction. He thought to himself, "How hard could this be, to write a story in 500 words or less? Why, I could finish the story in two shakes and a side of fries, thank you very much." He could even become famous for his use of sardonic euphemisms and signature plot twists. He would travel to foreign countries and seek girls… Fred suddenly snapped out of his reverie.

There was a number to call. Fred gingerly pulled his old phone out of his pocket. The cracked screen was threatening to break down entirely, the thin shards of toughened glass wedged together precariously as Fred carefully tapped in the number and set up an interview for 9 AM the following morning.

At five minutes after nine the next morning, Fred stepped over the threshold of the seedy office to meet his would-be boss, Mr. Dirkins. Fred was immediately uncomfortable as he could see that Mr. Dirkins had an obvious drinking problem. In fact, Fred suspected that Mr. Dirkins was half in the bag already. His nose was shot through with tiny capillaries and there were enough of them to give it a red patina that matched the color of his bloodshot eyes. The air was permeated with the scent of sour whiskey, no doubt borne on the wings of Mr. Dirkins' fetid breath.

"Fred Wilkins, is it?" asked Mr. Dirkins rhetorically. "I read some of your material and I must say that just one of your paragraphs is over the 500 word limit that defines our magazine. We're a publication for the new generation, people who can't get through a book to save their life. You've got to keep it short."

Just then there was a loud noise in the hall. The door burst open and in walked a man with a bologna sandwich and a gun. He threw the sandwich at Fred, pointed the gun at Mr. Dirkins and said,*

* Editor's note: *The story has exceeded 500 words and is no longer eligible for our magazine.*

BLUES FOR MYRTLE

Myrtle loved the blues. From the chug-chug of the big box guitar to the wailing sting of the thin-bodied electric, Myrtle could not get enough. It was the in-between notes she loved. The ones that got wedged in the cracks of the smoky soundscape, the ones that could pry up your emotions like a crowbar on a stuck plank and just as swiftly release you with their passing.

Myrtle was really digging this band.

On drums was Lester, a big Black guy with hooded eyes and loose jowls. He was playing with a beat so relaxed you could almost see the rhythms dragging themselves through sticky molasses on the way to the groove. Lester slouched on the drum throne, his left foot playing the sock cymbal almost tenderly while he popped the snare with an authoritative snap. His right foot pounded steadily on the bass drum and his other hand danced over the cymbals, a curious mockingbird looking for its mate.

Jamming on guitar was Slim, a tall lanky brown-skinned dude with slender fingers that looked like tender cherry birch twigs on a cool fall morning. His red electric guitar had an icepick tone that chipped through the back of your shoulders, thrilling its way to the tops of your toes. His face was scrunched in concentration, sweat streaming down in hot rivulets and sopping his shirt to the skin. Everytime he bent a high note into a sinuous wail his tongue would sneak out between his lips like a shy teenager on his first date.

Riffing on the organ was Bruce. He was a chubby Black guy with sausage-like fingers. They danced on the keyboard like busy ants, flirting to and fro with the black and white keys, teasing out choppy notes, staccato punctuations through the midnight air. His tone was dirty and badass, a growling beast prowling the sonic vista looking for unappreciative intruders to stomp.

Playing the upright bass was Arnie Finklestein, a pale cerebral fellow with horn-rimmed glasses and suspendered pants. He looked like a misfit but his bass told another story. She was his girl and she spun a tale of earthy significance, a bluesy narrative that evoked thoughts of primal pastimes yet to be experienced.

Myrtle was totally into this band. She really liked their intuitive sense, the way they played off of each other, igniting the music with a cohesive gestalt that really cooked. You could tell they loved it too, their grins jumping around the joint, infecting the crowd with joyous excitement.

The music wailed, dipping and soaring, a great black bird floating amongst the thermal currents of sound. Myrtle was dancing and could feel the vibrations throughout her entire body travelling down from her slender neck to her ample hips. She swayed to and fro, untired and eager, wanting more but knowing the night would eventually come to a close.

One o'clock in the morning came and went, and by two o'clock the band was on its last tune. The crowd had thinned out considerably, leaving a few stalwart blues junkies in its wake. The tune ended with the last note hanging in the sludgy air and ready to go to bed. The band reluctantly started its ritual of packing up and going home.

Lester broke down his cymbals one by one, slowly putting them away in their cases while nursing his last drink.

Slim took his guitar and put it away quickly, wrapping up the cords in a brusque manner so he could go to the bar and flirt with the bartender.

Bruce started the laborious process of disassembling the organ so he could load it onto his hand truck and wheel it out to the van.

But it was Arnie Finkelstein who took the most time of all. He loved his upright bass and he treated her with respect and dignity. He gently laid the bass on her side and wiped the neck down with a soft cloth, gently caressing the entire length of each string. He then put a little oil on the cloth and fastidiously began to polish the wooden body to a rich pulchritude, the rag gently teasing out the luster of the wood grain.

His adorations finished, Arnie picked up the soft case and began carefully putting it on the bass. He worked the covering over her hips, pulling it up gently and tenderly tucking the bass into it. He zipped her up slowly, the large zipper purring softly as it sealed her lower body, tracking purposefully around her hips and finally up her neck. Arnie stopped just short of the end and leaned close to the opening.

He took an appreciative breath and, leaning in just a little bit more, quietly whispered, "Good night Myrtle."

THE BABY IS SLEEPING

"Shhh, the baby is sleeping," whispered Jennifer. She was holding the tot in her arms as she opened the door. I immediately felt guilty for knocking.

"Sorry," I whispered back as I shusshed into the room. "I was in the neighborhood so I just popped in to ask you to remind John that we are playing disc golf tomorrow at noon."

"OK, I'll do it," whispered Jennifer as she moved her free arm in a fanning motion to indicate I should leave. As I was backing out, I felt a slight tickle in my sinuses that slowly crept down into my nose. It expanded into an itch and I tried valiantly to curb the inevitability of a loud messy sneeze. Just as I thought I had it under control, the tip of my nose went into overdrive and "aaatchooo" — a huge voluminous sneeze came thundering out. Jennifer looked at me in horror, then at the baby in her arms.

The baby's eyes immediately snapped open as it took a ridiculously deep breath and let out with a piercing "Waaaah." As soon as the cry was done the baby scrunched his eyes shut and took another impossibly deep breath.

"Waaaaugh," screamed the baby, the sound of which was a combination of siren and buzzsaw, a sonic needle that threatened to pierce my ears. I could tell by the exasperated look in Jennifer's eyes that the baby was just warming up.

"Eeeeaaaaagh," cried the baby, the sheer force of which caused snot to bubble out of his nose and a copious amount of drool to come out of his mouth.

"Yeeeeaaaagh," screamed the baby again in a tone not unlike the sound of a hundred fingernails screeching across a blackboard. The noise raised my hackles and my shoulders electrified in tension as another wail harpooned my skull and culminated in a blinding headache. Now the baby was warmed up. Its face turned bluish and it started to pump out shrieks like a demonized accordion. Jennifer cooed and tried to rock the baby into sleep ... anything to squelch this unholy cacophony.

Headache notwithstanding, I decided to stay and comfort both of them. Luckily my afternoon was free and so I waited the baby out, making small talk with Jennifer as the baby's wails subsided into whimpers and then finally it blessedly fell to sleep.

Outside, a FedEx van pulled up and I saw the upstairs neighbor excitedly come out to the curb. The FedEx guy unloaded three large boxes that were clearly branded in big letters — "Onkyo Home Theater Sound System." The driver then had the neighbor sign the manifest, got back into the van and sped off. The neighbor grabbed the largest box and with a thunk, thunk, thunk tromped up the outside stairs to his apartment directly above Jennifer's.

Jennifer cringed. The baby stirred, then opened its eyes as a large thump came down from the ceiling. The baby inhaled sharply.

The future did not look good.

BON VOYAGE

The customary amount of money to tip a waiter at a decent restaurant generally ranges from 15 to 20 percent of the entire bill, minus tax. That was just about the only thing the two planets had in common. An elite scouting party from the planet Arkon had secretly landed on Earth and made this observation.

After studying the occupants for over six months, the scouts came to the conclusion that the planet was unfit to be invaded. The Arkonists were a highly intelligent people. Their invasion strategy involved surreptitiously inserting themselves, both physically and culturally, into the mainstream of the targeted planet. Then over the course of approximately 500 years, they would breed profusely and their offspring would overwhelm the population of the planet.

However, the Arkonist council concluded that several of Earth's religions had already initiated this protocol and the planet was currently in the throes of imminent overpopulation. Additionally, the aliens realized that the people of Earth were too violent to be able to sustain any extended period of peace. So they made plans to leave Earth and head back to Arkon in order to regroup and take over another planet instead.

The 72 million-light-year trip to Earth had not been an entire loss. The Arkonists had collected a myriad of souvenirs, items deemed to be unique and amusing for their families back home. They appropriated the movies and reality TV shows such as "The Real Housewives of Beverly Hills" that they had so enjoyed watching, marveling at how the Earthlings, in their pitiful ignorance, could somehow have produced entertainment that was so utterly mesmerizing.

The Arkonists were also fascinated by the vehicles known as lowriders, agawk with the concept of a little truck that was basically undrivable due to the fact it could not navigate over minor irregularities such as speed bumps on the driving surface. Also, as a bonus, most of the lowriders were equipped with high-powered sound systems, curious devices that somehow rendered music unlistenable.

The aliens were also intrigued by the Earthlings' concept of fast food. This idea was something that might benefit their home planet because of its time-saving nature, something that mostly was not an Arkonist trait.

And lastly, they were enamored with social media

and its ability to connect the people of an entire planet together through a global system of computer networks.

The Arkonist captain smiled as the last of her crew walked up the ramp and boarded the ship. They were finally going home. The ramp was pulled up with some difficulty, hindered by the squeaky hinges that had rusted in the alien atmosphere of Earth. After making sure that everyone was settled in, the captain pushed the big red "Start" button on the main console. The ship's engine turned over reluctantly, finally sputtering fitfully to life. The captain let it warm up a little then pushed the green "Go" button on the console and the ship slowly rose through the atmosphere, its engine billowing clouds of black smoke that hung on the ground like sulking teenagers at a 7-Eleven.

Tucked in the bushes 492 kilometers away, the clandestine observation crew of the planet Zirgon celebrated enthusiastically. They chuckled heartily as they watched the Arkonist ship lift off with all the goods they had planted. In about 300 short years the Arkonists will have stupefied themselves into a vulnerable state. A state ripe for invasion, a service that the Zirgonians were more than happy to provide.

In the meantime, they had their hands full. The Earth was ready to be taken over soon, probably just after the next election. A couple of birds chirped happily nearby as the Zirgonians opened their first bottle of champagne and toasted to their good fortune.

LAUGHTER IS THE BEST MEDICINE

"You are genuinely funny," said the flushed anesthesiologist to Dr. Elwin A. Ziggle, Head Neurosurgeon at the Mustard Clinic in Poughkeepsie, New York.

He smiled as he continued his scrubbing protocol for the 6 AM operation on the brain of one Brian Flossman who was currently sporting a golf-ball-sized tumor buried deep in his temporal lobe. Dr. Ziggle focused his mind on the procedure, methodically going through each step in his head.

He was pleased with the morning's agenda, particularly about the first step of the operation — a craniotomy which he had passed off to Dr. Hank Huber, a youthful up-and-comer who was four-and-a-half years into the clinic's neurosurgery residency program. Dr. Ziggle never liked doing craniotomies, he found the process of drilling out an eight-centimeter chunk of bone in order to expose the brain a bit boring.

The entire team conscientiously assembled in the operating theater and a sterile hush slowly infected the room. Dr. Ziggle nodded for the procedure to begin. The stainless steel tools were nested neatly next to the operating table in sterile packs, cold precursors of the complex procedure to come. The patient's head had been duly shaved and prepared, the newly exposed skin gleaming impatiently under the powerful lights of the OR. The team hovered around the anesthetized body as Dr. Huber took a long measured breath, picked up his instrument, and began drilling his way into Brian's skull.

The drill whined eagerly as the acrid odor of smoking bone occupied the air with the olfactory equivalent of a piece of chalk screeching on a crisp chalkboard. A needling sense of discomfort sinuated its way to the innocent composures of the fresh-faced interns observing from the back of the room.

The incision complete, Dr. Huber gingerly inserted a bladed tool into Brian's skull and levered it downward, causing the bone to lift up and leave the brain exposed. Satisfied with Dr. Huber's deft undertaking, Dr. Ziggle moved close to the table and assessed the situation. The fibrous white sheen of the meninges glistened wetly as the surgeon poked it with his finger and probed for clues that might enhance the elaborate procedure. As he fingered the slimy ridges of the cerebrum, his mind wandered back to the anesthesiologist's statement and wondered what she had meant by it. *Was she trying to send him a signal?* She knew he was married, so why would she say such a thing? He tried to focus his attention back on the operation but it was difficult, so much so that he didn't notice the small pocket of gas forming in his lower colon. As the pocket grew alarmingly in size, he realized it was too late to corral the pressure of the gas as it traveled downward towards its exit. The gas embarrassingly snuck through Dr. Ziggle's sphincter and manifested itself as a tiny fart that peeped into the room like a shy puppy. The team tittered covertly, not realizing that the smell was going to become so bad as to be laughable.

The head nurse was the first to crack and she let out a surprised guffaw with a healthy snort behind it. The snort triggered a landslide of laughter from the crew and boomeranged back to the poor doctor. He unwillingly started to laugh too and in doing so lost control of the remaining gas in his bowels, letting out a huge raspberry that greased the hair back on his assistant's head. The smell hit the back wall like a typhoon and, choking, one of the snarky students pulled off his latex glove, inflated it with his mouth and let it go. The sound of the glove blattering across the room sounded exactly like the doctor's fart and caused the anesthesiologist to go into such a violent spasm of laughter that she accidentally pulled out the endotracheal tube that had been down the patient's mouth and let go of the valve on her continuous-flow anesthesia machine. She doubled up in tears, desperately looking for the end of the tube and gasping for oxygen as the entire theater went wild.

With the flow of gas from the anesthesia machine interrupted, the patient suddenly opened his eyes and sat up sharply, the flap of skull dangling precariously by his head.

Shocked by the raucous melee, he blurted out, "What's so goddamn funny?!"

Instantly the entire room plunged into a horrified silence, punctuated only by the unflappable sound of the EKG machine.

A few seconds of electronic beeps took their time going by, then the doctor solemnly reached his hand out to the patient and said, "Dude, pull my finger!"

TRIXIE

Period. The end of the sentence hung in the air, an unwelcome reminder that things were not going well with the relationship.

"If that's the case," replied Charlie, "I'll give the marriage counselor a call today."

"I'd really appreciate that," said Sheila, and the implied threat of separation left the room.

The dog thumped her tail on the wood floor and looked at the couple with hopeful eyes. No, Trixie didn't understand what was going on between Charlie and Sheila, rather she was thinking about the treats in the jar and how long it had been since she'd had one. As if reading her mind, Sheila got up and walked to the jar. "Treat, Trixie, it's time for a treat!" She fished out a bacon-flavored goodie and dangled it just over Trixie's head.

"Sit, now sit … no, sit. C'mon sit … oh, that's a good girl," said Sheila as she let go of the treat. Trixie caught it with a snap and took it to her bed next to Charlie. He watched appreciatively as Trixie played with the treat for a second, then swallowed it whole.

"God, I love that dog," thought Charlie to himself.

Sheila too looked at Trixie admiringly and thought to herself "God, I love that dog."

The marriage had been going great for about seven years until the Covid-19 virus hit and blew things apart. They had lost their jobs during the lockdown and were forced to spend a lot of time together. Too much time. The dog had been the saving grace, giving them comfort and solace through the long days and nights.

"Would you like another treat, Trixie?" asked Charlie even though he knew the answer was yes, had always been yes, and always would be yes. He got up, but on his way to the treat jar remembered the leftover bone that had been in the fridge for a while. It was just about to turn bad so Charlie took it out and put it in Trixie's dish. She started to gnaw on it with relish as Charlie watched and thought "God, I love that dog."

Sheila looked on appreciatively and thought to herself, "God, I love that dog."

Both Charlie and Sheila had been fully vaccinated for over a month, and although the economy was getting back into gear, they were still jobless. The uncertainty of their future lay scattered about the room, shards of worry caused by bills and broken things.

As the day wore on, Charlie couldn't stop thinking

about their relationship. After all, he had agreed to see the counselor … wasn't that enough to show that he was willing to make things right?

And Sheila thought about the dog, about how Trixie had an easy life with two good people who loved her so much. All she had to do was eat, sleep, pee, poop, and love them. Trixie's love was unconditional, given freely and in great quantities. Why couldn't Charlie be like that? After all, he had the eating, sleeping, peeing, and pooping part down. But not the loving part.

She fed the dog, noting that the special blend of ground turkey, veggies and rice was something Charlie always made. At least he was good for something. Sighing, she pulled two chicken pot pies out of the oven. She put them on plates, and brought them to the table, calling out to Charlie, "Food's ready," as she eased into her chair.

Charlie came into the dining room and sat down in front of his magazine, mumbled a thanks and tucked into his food. Sheila was glad he did. She had her book in front of her and would rather read than converse with her husband.

They ate in silence, the bleakness of their future weighing them down, a lead anchor in a flimsy boat. Sheila made it through two-thirds of her chicken pot pie, then put the plate on the floor and watched as Trixie slurped it up. Charlie did the same thing and Trixie's belly swelled up from all the food, almost as tight as the goat skin on a bongo drum. Trixie licked the last vestiges of chicken pot pie from the plate and padded off into the bedroom.

Bereft of the dog's stabilizing presence, Charlie did the dishes, methodically cleaning them as he pondered the question of how much longer this could last. Their relationship was proceeding by rote and about the only thing they did together was watch television after dinner. Charlie could hear Trixie snoring in the bedroom as he sat down on the couch next to Sheila, grabbed the remote and turned on the TV. Sheila put her book down and looked at the screen. She so wanted to love Charlie. She worked hard on it but her efforts never gave her the feeling she had when she loved the dog.

"The dog," thought Charlie, "maybe she knows the answer to the riddle of love. She sleeps in the middle of the bed, soaking it up. How does she put all our differences away and love ... just simple, easy flowing love?"

Wordlessly, Charlie and Sheila went to bed. Trixie was in her usual spot in the middle, stretched out fully on her back, her stomach softly gurgling. Charlie and Sheila eased into the bed so as not to disturb her. They went through their "Good nights," wishing each other well. They had lost track of their love in a sea of familiarity.

Soon they both fell into a deep sleep. Trixie's stomach

rumbled and suddenly contracted in a heaving spasm, forcing the dog to throw up on the bed. The couple slept on. Unfazed, Trixie ate all the vomit back up, licked her lips and returned to sleep. As the trio slept peacefully, a question rose up from under the covers.

"What was going to happen with Charlie and Sheila?"

A cool breeze whispered through the room. Trixie's stomach gurgled again.

Only love had the answer.

TV PICTURE TUBE

The TV picture tube shoots a beam of hackneyed light through the air. A child absorbs the information like a damp sponge, the low-grade flickering playing out in reverse on his skin.

Somewhere on the beach a wave licks the sand, a bird creases the sky, and the wind tells a story. It's a story of love — a whispered song of energy kept, its unseen power abated for human consumption, a trifle to be experienced in an infinitely small dose. Because humans fail to understand the raw power of the universe, that for each grain of sand of the beach there is a star fusing its neurons into great gouts of energy, dispersing itself through infinite space.

The child's eyes are glazed with a viscous gel, the liquidity of which lubricates the clear orbs and facilitates the retinal intake of the TV picture tube. The child shifts his position slightly, giving his long-seated gluteal area a respite from the moribund hours on the couch. On screen, an asthmatic Chihuahua slaps a stupid cat across the face as he exhorts, "You eeediot", his eyeballs popping out in apoplexy. The child laughs with glee as the play of light from the TV picture tube infects his psyche with moronic aplomb. He moves his body slightly closer to the electronic emanations as the mid-rangey tones from the speaker insinuate themselves into his brain.

Outside, an ever-present cosmic play is unfolding. The hand of a storm squeezes thunder into rain as nightfall smothers the final gasp of daylight. And the suns beyond earth's atmosphere burn, their superheated plasmas firing into the void.

The TV picture tube persists with its saga, thoroughly warmed by the hours of continuous use. It is in its element, oozing out a mucilaginous web of useless information. The child is drooling slightly, his jaws relaxing in familiar stupor as the hours tick off the clock. A singing box of laundry detergent cavorts its way across the screen as the child's mother steps into the room.

"Arthur," she says, "It's time for bed." The child can barely move, his zombie-like lethargy leaching into the sofa. The TV picture tube continues its stupefying message as the mother levers the child off the couch and, coaxing him onto his unsteady feet, leads him into his bedroom. The child, fully clothed, flops onto the bed, and the mother, too tired to care, tucks him in sloppily. In the other room, the TV picture tube continues to flicker, its message to the empty confines of the room unaffected by the lack of an audience.

And outside, outside of the electronically sealed box of a home, the universe rages on.

A TURN OF HABIT

Mildred became a nun on July 23rd, in the year of our Lord, 1983. She was a little wacky and becoming a nun didn't stop her from being so. She wore rainbow leggings under her black-and-white habit and a neon-colored top to match.

Mildred loved decaffeinated coffee. Now some may argue that decaf is not really coffee, but to Mildred that was just a bunch of hooey. The smell of fresh coffee thrilled her almost as much as her commitment to Jesus Christ, hallowed be thy name. Mildred was aware that loving her coffee was a sin, but according to her Mother Superior, it was a pardonable sin, one which Mildred justified as even more pardonable since the coffee she drank was decaffeinated and, according to some, not really coffee.

One sunny morning, Mildred was assigned to run some errands for the convent. She felt a slight ripple of delight thinking about her day because she could get a mid-morning coffee in between her chores. Admittedly she felt some guilt but quickly forgave herself for the much anticipated minor transgression.

Her first stop was at Costco to pick up some toilet paper and cream cheese for the Sisters. She also had rounds to make for the affiliated charities that belonged to The Order of Saint Benedict Arnold. Everything went smoothly and it was time for her little break. There was a certain place she liked to go — Frank's Coffee Shop, located on the corner of Smith and Wesson streets. She grew secretly excited as she stepped over the threshold of the shop. Her large nose instantly tracked the smell of grinding coffee and led her to an empty seat at the counter.

Ricky Stimble worked the counter at Frank's. He was in his second year of vocational school studying to be an auto mechanic. Lately he had been preoccupied with the specter of an upcoming test and wasn't sure if he had the intellectual skills to pass it. Thus it came to be that when he made the pot of decaffeinated coffee he mistakenly made it with regular coffee. Freshly ground regular coffee. Ricky glanced at Mildred. He had noticed her before, I mean how many times do you see a nun in a coffee shop?

Ricky came over and Mildred ordered a cup of de-caffeinated coffee. Ricky nodded and said, "You came at the right time, I just made a fresh pot."

Mildred smiled and replied, "Thank you."

Ricky grabbed the pot and poured her a cup. Mildred's anticipation perked up and her nose joyfully inhaled the smell of the hot, rich, black liquid. Mildred stirred in some cream and sugar and took a sip. Instantly her taste buds woke up and started dancing the Electric Slide. The flavor soothed her with the comfort of all being well in her world, and the small pang of guilt in the back of her mind sheepishly tiptoed away. Mildred opened her catechism and reviewed the principles that had guided her to her faith. Presently she felt a little thrill of voltage as the caffeine strode deeper into her brain and said "Hello there!"

She took another few sips. Her heart started pumping faster and a smile crept onto her lips like a sneaky marmot. She was feeling good, powerfully good. In fact, Mildred had never felt this way before. She began to suspect that Ricky had given her a cup of caffeinated coffee. She drained her cup with an eager slurp and ordered another.

She took the first sip from the fresh cup and definitely felt a stimulating zoink. The zoink dashed through her veins and opened them up like fire hoses. Little jolts of electricity shot through her fingertips as her pupils dilated and her eyelids began to twitch now and again from the caffeine rush. The increase of light hit her cortex and exploded it into little slivers of excitement, each piece piercing her ennui with the gleam of unfettered optimism. Her knees knocked like a ramshackle jalopy blasting uphill and her toes waggled with spry eccentricity.

Mildred finished her cup and a huge wave of euphoria propelled her into a standing position. She paid her tab and shot out the door purposefully, her habit billowing behind her like a shadow high on cocaine.

The brilliant sunlight hit her and Mildred's face lit up with a beatific smile. She skipped three times, stopped abruptly and spread her arms out in a cross-like fashion. She looked up to the sky and shouted at the top of her lungs, "That's it God, I'm switching to real coffee now!"

BLANK PAGE MEDITATION

Please seat yourself in a comfortable chair, bare feet flat on the floor. Close your eyes.

Picture the connection of your feet to the earth. Gradually expand that awareness and surround yourself with openness. Focus that openness towards your heart and flow yourself to the great inside.

Be there, then open your eyes. Look at this page.

Bring your awareness into the page, breathing out and in. On each in-breath, bring your awareness deeper into the page, deeper and deeper until you arrive at the molecular level. Picture yourself between the ink and the page, observing that there is no mass in this atomic space, only vibration.

The page is blank under the ink, its whiteness defined by the purity of your observation. Stay there in the between. Breathe.

Let your awareness insert itself within the confines of the page, the borders of which are sharp and clear. Be the page, infinitely blank.

Observe and breathe. Observe and breathe.

When you are ready, draw yourself into a tiny point and look up at the period of the previous sentence that is floating above you. Let yourself expand through the ink of that period, leaving the blankness of the page under you. As you grow, look down and see the page as two layers, one of ink and the other of blank paper.

Let this knowledge infuse itself into your chest from the heart, then from your heart into your extremities.

Gently close your inner eyes and become aware of your outer surroundings. See the room and cultivate your gratitude for ten breaths.

Your blank page meditation is now complete.

If you enjoyed this meditation, please fill out the survey on the back of this page and send $6.95 to Swami Whassumatuh, 1969 Frittlewitz Ave., Rye, New York 10580. Also note the two-for-one coupon underneath for the next lecture in the series entitled *"This Page Isn't Actually Blank"*.

Thank you for completing our popular "Blank Page Meditation".

In order to better serve our customers, please fill out this survey and send to: Swami Whassumatuh, 1969 Frittlewitz Ave., Rye, New York 10580. Your donation of $6.95 is humbly appreciated.

1. Were you uncomfortable during the meditation at any time?
   ❑ No   ❑ Yes   If "Yes", too bad.

2. Have you at any time been commited to an insane asylum?
   ❑ No   ❑ Yes   If "Yes", you've probably don't need to meditate.

3. Do you ever worry at night that a cat will come to your pillow and suck your breath out while you sleep?
   ❑ No   ❑ Yes   If Yes, me too!

4. Which allergy would you choose if you had to pick one?
   ❑ Gluten ❑ Peanut ❑ I'd rather die!

5. Do you get nervous when a doctor dons a rubber glove during a physical examination?
   ❑ Yes ❑ No, I rather look forward to what may happen next.

✂ *CLIP 'N SAVE!!!* ✂

2 for 1 COUPON

This coupon entitles the bearer to purchase two publications of Swami Whassumatuh's popular teaching "This Page Isn't Actually Blank" for the price of one.

Please note: Offer void in Arkansas and parts of New Jersey

THE ANT AND THE OCEAN

A turgid flap of atmosphere unbuttoned itself from a fallow sky, Slowly, a medium-sized ball dripped out and landed moistly on the ground below. A grackle bird flew by backwards, its recessive honk dopplering into soft resonance. The ball, sticky with dirt, rolled itself to a nearby anthill. A sleepy ocean barked in the distance.

Slowly, a pair of curious antennae vacated the hole at the top of the anthill. Intrigued, the rest of the ant pushed away a sandwich and crawled out, inquisitively pausing at the ball. The ant looked up and saw the flap slowly congealing back into the sky. A sullen weirdness gripped the ant and, smelling the tang of salt from the ocean, it headed off in that direction. A mustard-like slab of dirt sloughed off the ball.

The ant perambulated its way seaward, cutting a rhythmic swath through the hope-encrusted air. The ocean was imperfectly still, like the meditation of a monk with hemorrhoids. The ant continued its journey, wistfully thinking about the cool embrace of the ocean's deepness.

The ball deflated itself with a hiss of resignation and became inconsequential to the story. Nearby another smattering of inconsequence sneezed appreciatively.

The ant trudged on, its eyes blinking from the heat of the noonday sun. The ocean continued its stillness, its mass calling the ant like the moon calls the ocean. Overheated, the ant shivered with anticipation as the thought of the ocean's acceptance winnowed its way through the ant's brain. It crested a small hill, dirt gradually changing to sand as the ant spied the vastness of the ocean. Left, left, left, right, right, right, the ant's twiggy legs picked up their rhythm. As it sniffed the increasingly salty air, the ant was surprised at how easy moving had become and the beat of its tiny heart eased to a slower cadence. A wisp of cloud winked at the sun as the ant finally reached the water's edge.

"Love," said the ocean to the ant, "All is love."

The ant stepped into the ocean, gradually becoming immersed enough to start swimming.

"All is love," sang the sun to the universe as the ant dog-paddled its way seaward.

The ant felt at peace, the three words resonating with purposeful wisdom as the ant continued its way towards infinity.

A soft breeze woke up and pushed the ant further in

the direction of the All.

Excited for its future, the ant thought to itself, "What a glorious day for a swim."

ANOTHER HAND IN THE SPITOON

It was a lonely road. Lonely because the road was straight and I could see that there were no cars coming from miles away. Lonely because in the shimmering heat the long stretch of blacktop seemed to go nowhere. There wasn't a point in walking anymore. I set my bag down and sat heavily on top of it, wondering if the next vehicle could be my ride.

A half an hour later I saw a silver wink in the distance and although it was distorted in the heat, I could tell there was a car approaching. I slowly stood up and shook the rumples out of my clothes. The car became a truck as I could now see its features. It was a battered old Dodge sporting a mottled mint-green paint job. My thumb was out and I could hear the crippled exhaust of a loose muffler rattling by as the truck down-shifted and came to a squeaky halt just past me. I walked quickly to the vehicle, a small flicker of worry flashing in my head as I spotted a well-worn confederate flag sticker on the rear bumper. I pulled open the battered door and slid into the truck, putting the bag down by my feet.

The driver looked at me and flashed a smile, his nicotine teeth showing some gaps in his crooked grin.

"I'm heading to Houston," he said, gunning the truck forward as I shut the door.

"Me too, thanks!" I responded.

The truck cab had a sour smell of tobacco and spit. I glanced at the driver as he changed gears. He looked like he was on the heavy side of fifty, his hairy stomach protruding from the bottom of his T-shirt and spilling over his waist. His red neck was dirty all the way up to his hairline and his sideburns were almost indistinguishable from the week-old brown stubble on his face. His hair was dyed a sticky yellow and he turned to me and said, "My name's Randy."

"Really? Mine is too," I said to him as I thought to myself how can two such very different people have the same name.

There was a large well-used spittoon behind the stick shift. My stomach did a turn as I focused on its condition. Large specks of dried phlegm stuck on the metal sides of the container. Lines of old saliva had drooled their way down the transmission hump, looking like an encrusted spiderweb as they drizzled out onto the floor of the truck.

"Got any chew?" asked Randy as he instinctively patted his empty pants pockets. A thin trickle of saliva slid out of the corner of his mouth in anticipation of an affirmative answer from me.

"No, I don't," I answered.

"Damn," he responded, "I guess I'll just have to make do." With that he reached his greasy hand into the spittoon and fished around for an expectorated plug of tobacco. His fingers explored their way hungrily through the skinned slime as they tried to differentiate the various viscosities. Finally they found a congealed mass not un-like rotted oyster meat and pinched it out of the spittoon. Randy's mouth opened and as his hand hovered over it, the truck hit a bump, knocking the wad onto the seat between us. The slug landed with a fleshy splat and little bits of splosh flicked onto my pants. I stared at the heap in disgust. It was mildly translucent, a greenish-black color flecked with tiny bits of squiggly blood. There were some delicate gossamer strings of lung matter suspended in the congealment and my stomach heaved as I tried to contain myself.

Randy said, "Don't worry about it, happens all the time," as he tried to pick up the mass with his beefy hand. I saw his disgusting nails squeeze the plug, its juicy brown overflow trickling down his fingers as he deftly put it into his mouth and started to chew. A cold silence froze the air between us and I knew with dead certainty that this did not bode well. I felt myself overwhelmed with anxiety as

I noticed the radio playing patriotic country music, its trebly output assaulting me with redneck vigor. *Had it been on all this time and I never noticed?* The tension between us became unbearable and I stiffened as Randy put his wet hand on my kneecap and squeezed really hard. A white hot lance of pain ran through my body as he asked me, "Would you like to try a slug?"

I slowly closed my eyes in desperation and replied, "Sure, why not?" Then I reached my hand into the spittoon.

THE MAN WHO KNEW EVE

My name is Adam and I'm an irascible son of a bitch… figuratively speaking of course, being the first man and all that. Now I know you're going to go into palpitations when you hear my story but hey, this might be fiction. If you don't like it you can stuff it where the sun don't shine.

As you know I got my rib ripped out by the Old Man so that he could make me a woman. Not only was that painful but the recovery was hell. Don't get me wrong, Eve was a beautiful woman, no complaints in that department, but life was a bit simpler before all the hullabaloo started.

Prior to Mr. Snaky Wakey fouling things up, the situation was fairly uncomplicated in the garden. A typical day, and believe me, they were all typical, would've gone something like this. Eve and I would get up late after lounging around naked all morning. I'd get out of bed first, shaking the leaves and grass out of my hair and brush my teeth. Kidding, this was Eden, we didn't get cavities so no brushing necessary. Eve would pop out of the sack next, looking all radiant and pure. We would gaze at each other affectionately; we didn't talk much since there wasn't much to talk about. We'd eat some breakfast, usually fruit and nuts, then wander around till lunch. By then we'd be near the vegetable patch so we'd pick some lettuce and stuff then head back to the hut for lunch. After lunch we would look at each other affectionately again and then we'd go our own ways, each of us blissfully happy in our solitude. A couple of hours before sundown I'd start looking around for a chicken to strangle, you know, get some protein for supper. When I'd get back Eve would be happy to prepare the food while I'd get the fire going. We would enjoy our repast then take a little night stroll before going to bed. We had a very peaceful lifestyle in those days and I could sum it up in one word — boring. I guess you could say we had it all but to tell you the truth I just wasn't satisfied. Call it a tickle or a little scratching in the back of my head but there was something about Eve that just felt missing.

You all know about that fateful day when the snake talked Eve into biting that apple but I'll tell you what, that apple would've gotten eaten sooner or later, snake or not. I mean think about it, here we were with everything we could possibly need, bored to tears, and there's one thing the Old Man said we couldn't touch. It's the most beautiful tree in the garden, with a gorgeous trunk supporting branches just loaded with red shiny apples. We weren't allowed to touch the tree or the apples on the ground but we could sure see and smell them. Forget what I said about our idyllic life, we were obsessed with those freaking apples.

So Eve and I took a bite of the apple, no big thing, right? Wrong. That apple virtually exploded in my head, the flavor so intense that I could barely keep myself from stuffing the whole thing into my face. That apple was so juicy, just dripping with flavor and when I looked up, Eve was looking at me with a funny expression on her face. It was, as I later found out, the look of embarrassment. But I'll tell you right now, she looked hot. She ran over to the fig tree, grabbed some leaves and used them as skimpy coverings on the parts of her body that were different than mine and, guess what, she looked even hotter. I mean it was like the same thing with the apple, you know, forbidden fruit and all that. Meanwhile, I'm going half crazy with craving and all of a sudden, schwing, my body is doing something it's never done before. I carefully walked over to Eve, got real close, looked her in the eye and said, "I'd like to get to know you better."

She shyly looked at me and said "Me too."

So I knew her. Man, did I ever know her. I knew her back and forth, I knew her sideways and upside down,

I knew her all night long. And lucky for you that I did because you wouldn't be here if I hadn't worked it out. So that's my story.

Things changed after that. Eve would get bitchy sometimes and I, like I said before, became irascible. We had some good times and some bad times but basically we just wanted a whole bunch more stuff. Sometimes I would feel some peace and clarity, kind of like what we had before the apple, but back then things were so perfect that they just became monotonous. So the kids grew up and we all had some swinging times together. Don't think about it too much or you'll get all moral on me. The times were what they were and we did what we did. I don't feel like we did anything wrong, especially the apple part. It's kind of like it was meant to be. So put that in your pipe and smoke it. And if you ever get that longing to be in the garden of Eden, just remember, it ain't all cracked up to what it's supposed to be.

MONEY AND THE PIG

Jeremy was an odd-looking kid. Skinny as a kosher hotdog, he had long gangly arms and a stiff neck. Jeremy was eleven and like any other active kid he had seen his fair share of bumps and bruises. His stiff neck was the result of an accident with a pogo stick that had been quite a bit more than a mishap. He had gone down hard on the pavement and suffered a hairline fracture in his neck that consequently limited his motion above the shoulders. Since he was thin and stiff the kids at school took to calling him Pogo and Jeremy brooked it with a resolute loneliness. His solitude wasn't so bad as to be dysfunctional but Jeremy carried the weight of the taunts like a bag of sloppy cement on his shoulders. To compensate, Jeremy developed quite an active imagination and preferred to live in his inner world.

For his eleventh birthday Jeremy's parents had given him a really nice piggy bank. It was rather large and made out of white glazed ceramic. It had shiny and smooth skin with a slot on top of its back. Underneath, the belly was glossy with no opening to get the money out. This was a one-way piggy bank. Jeremy loved his new friend and named him Skoosh. Skoosh was a happy pig and he loved money, so one day he asked Jeremy what he was saving up for.

"I don't know," replied Jeremy.

Skoosh rolled his eyes and said, "Well, we'll think of something."

Jeremy let out an uninterested sigh and fed Skoosh a few pennies. Skoosh tried out a number of possibilities on Jeremy to no avail and then he hit upon a bright idea.

"Hey, how about a rocket set?" asked Skoosh.

Jeremy's eyes lit up like a pair of silver dollars as he conjured up the image of shooting a rocket into outer space.

"Yeah, good, that's a great idea. Gee, thanks," said Jeremy.

He grew inspired. He asked his parents for odd jobs. He researched what kind of model rockets and launchers were best and found a kit that he really liked. It was a good one but expensive and Jeremy knew he was going to have to save up for a while. He got a paper route and started washing the neighbors' cars. The coins grew rarer as Jeremy took to slipping more and more bills into Skoosh's slot. Skoosh was happy and told Jeremy that the bills tickled him. Jeremy laughed and fed him some more money. Skoosh winked at him and rolled his eyes vertically like two twirling pennies.

"That rocket is going to be very cool," said Skoosh.

Six months went by and Jeremy was happy feeding Skoosh the money. Skoosh was over the moon with joy, his belly filling up with sundry currency, the feeling of fulfillment infusing him happily with richness.

One day Jeremy was putting in some bills and he noticed that there was only a little space left; Skoosh was beginning to fill up.

"Hey Skoosh," Jeremy asked, "What's going to happen when you get full?"

Skoosh looked at him directly and said, "Why, that will be the best day ever because I'll be full of money. My life will then be complete and you will break me open so that your wish will come true."

Dumbfounded, Jeremy looked at Skoosh. When he had heard the word "break", big red letters popped up in his brain.

"What do you mean?" asked Jeremy.

"Well, the only way to get to the money is to break me open. That's the way I was designed. It's okay, I want you to be happy," Skoosh replied.

Jeremy couldn't fathom Skoosh's meaning, he wanted Skoosh to be around. Skoosh was his only friend and the thought of his absence was unbearable.

Jeremy grew sad and started working sporadically, subsequently putting less money into Skoosh's slot. Skoosh was also becoming more unhappy as the days went by and the incoming money dwindled to almost nothing. Jeremy sensed Skoosh's sadness and the two didn't share the joy in being together they once had. One day as Jeremy was trying to fit a dollar bill into Skoosh's stuffed body he asked him if what he had said about being happy when he was broken was really true.

Skoosh's eyes brightened, a spark kindling his gaze as he told Jeremy, "Yes, yes, of course it's true. This is what I want to do for you. I love you Jeremy, and my goal in life is to give myself to you so you can live your life knowing true love."

Jeremy looked at Skoosh in a new light. He finally understood the meaning of what Skoosh was saying. He felt something shift inside him as he realized that Skoosh's destiny was to make him happy. Jeremy looked down at the floor and there he spotted the penny that he had been too lazy to pick up over the past month.

He polished it off slowly and said,"Skoosh, this is the last bit of money I can put in you. I love you too and I want you to be fulfilled".

With that he slid the penny into the slot, working the coin into the last available space.

"Thank you," said Skoosh with a warm sigh. He

closed his eyes and became still.

The next day Jeremy came into the room with his dad's hammer. Skoosh was as inanimate as all the other objects in the room and Jeremy, his eyes filled with tears, broke Skoosh into pieces as gently as he could. The money spilled out, coins clinking and bills fluttering to the floor. Jeremy gingerly picked out the pieces of Skoosh and put them in a box that he placed in an open drawer. He then gathered up the money, counted it and was satisfied knowing that there was enough for his rocket set. He closed his eyes and heard Skoosh's final words of gratitude in his heart. He slid the drawer shut and went downstairs.

Jeremy's rocket set arrived three weeks later. He didn't quite know what to expect as he opened the box but his heart leapt in wonder as he saw all the parts and pieces that were going to be his rocket. Something clicked in his mind right then, and like a completed puzzle he understood the form and function of each piece in the box. It was magic and he started assembling the rocket without looking at the manual. Jeremy's fingers seemed to have a mind of their own, and right then he knew without a shadow of a doubt that he was meant to be an engineer. He assembled the rocket with patience, understanding, and loving care. He adjusted the primitive guidance system. He took his time putting together the launch assembly, each part a new discovery that sent waves of excitement through his body. It took him a full week to complete the project and his newfound skill showed. The rocket was beautiful, every detail minutely completed, its flight balance perfectly aligned and ready for maximum altitude.

Finally the launch day arrived. Jeremy came home from school and excitedly gathered his things. As he readied his kit he was suddenly enveloped in a wave of gratitude. He could feel Skoosh's sacrifice in his heart like a warm sun ready to burst forth with uncontainable love. He understood what a great honor it was to have fulfilled Skoosh's destiny and how it had turned his life around.

He walked out the door and down the steps with the rocket in a big box. As he reached the sidewalk he saw two kids from school coming towards him.

They smirked at him and the bigger one chided, "What do you have in that box, Pogo?"

Jeremy heard the words and smiled as he felt Skoosh's gift in his heart. Pogo was a lifetime ago.

CHAPTER TWO

"If money is the root of all evil, I'm getting nicer every day."

- Earl

MY FRIENDS

The rain came down softly, almost slowly, if that were even possible. Swollen drops gathered on the lip of the eave, expanding until they could no longer contain themselves, then spilling over the edge, lemmings tumbling off a cliff.

The dog was splayed out on his big bed, his eyes the only part of him that were animated, maneuvering in their sockets as they took in the space of the room. The dog could see the author in the corner, naked and gibbering. The author was physically okay, he had just put himself in this position so he could write the word "gibbering."

He lived to write words — fat words, skinny words, words one's brain could chew on. Like "lugubrious." That word just plodded around on its sad meaty legs, its pitiful demeanor perpetuated by neglect and underuse. Or "flamboyant," a word that said aloud just announces itself to the world with carefree abandon, a lark japing in the crisp noonday sun. And "exorbitant". Oh, that was a massive word, a chest swollen with air, breath held high and tight, then let out in a whoosh of excessive relief.

Yes, the author loved his words. He would visit them nightly in their leather-bound world, the pages of which contained alphabetically delineated neighborhoods, some more crowded than others. Neighborhoods in which the words lived in peace and harmony. Usually the author would visit two or three words in a typical evening. To find them, he would open the dictionary and pick a P, or sight an S, regard an R, or view a V, examine an E or behold a B, it didn't matter, the world of words was his oyster.

The words he focused on loved to be descried and he liked exploring their meanings and inflections. Fascinated with their genealogy, he would dive into their roots and peruse their diverse provenances with relish. And when he had fully ingurgitated a word, he would visit its relatives living in his thesaurus, pursuing their diversity with zest.

This was when the author was at his happiest, ensconced in his writing chair in the pre-dawn hours of the day, his dog snoring softly by his side and passing gas.

And so, if you encounter the author in a corner or two, naked and gibbering, take heart, for he is blithesome and possibly just a bit berserk. Don't be shy, park yourself on a chair and talk to him. Be patient, if you stay long enough he'll come around.

DARK STAIN

A bank of ominous clouds hung somberly over the broken horizon, heralds of the violence to come. Sharp hooves of a sweat-lathered horse struck the ground furiously as the grim-faced rider pushed the animal to its limit. His long black cape swirled behind him like spilled ink, the sweep of it blotting the air with its muscular billowing.

Perched on a gnarled branch, a midnight raven cawed viciously into the forest as it watched the assassin ride. The moon cast a feeble ray towards the journey, a cold light that was no match for the viscous fog that lay on the road below.

Alizar had traveled this road many times and his familiarity with it eased the confusion of the darkened way. His thoughts were focused on the mission, the purpose of which was to find and retrieve the ampule of rare liquid that his master needed. The directive was absolute, yet Alizar reluctantly entertained a rogue thought that cast doubt upon its execution. A festering hate rumbled inside his gut as Alizar ruminated on the man's endless mandates that forced him to kill in order to do his bidding.

He rode on and time turned the night into day as the heavy fog parted for the tired horse. Alizar's instructions were very clear. He was to ride into the village and find the alchemist who had painstakingly concocted the liquid and bottled it in a small glass vial. The liquid was magical, its property ravenously desired by the master because of its ability to render thoughts into reality and to make the fleeting nature of them permanent and something magnificent to behold. The liquid was in great demand by many people and selfishly kept by the alchemist who commanded an exorbitant price from whomever he chose to sell it.

That was about to change as Alizar reached his destination and dismounted from his horse. He spotted five guards in the distance. He noted the fortified building, heavy and private, the mass of which forbade access without permission. The assassin had that permission by his side, a blade that had sharply penetrated many unsuspecting victims of his master's ire. Alizar watched quietly as a single guard separated from the contingent in front of the building and approached him dutifully.

"What business do you have here?" said the guard as he stepped into the assassin's death zone.

In the blink of an eye and quietly as such, Alizar swiftly drew his dagger and plunged it into the leather armor that protected the stomach of the unsuspecting guard. The razor-sharp blade easily pierced the tough hide and slid into the soft flesh within, fatally injuring the guard as the repulsive stink of his bowel escaped into the dead air. Alizar turned his back to the guards and casually reached over to his horse. He withdrew a massive sword from the oversized leather scabbard bound to the saddle. The sword's preposterous weight made it uncomfortable to bear but Alizar liked having the weapon close at hand for a circumstance like this.

The guards, finally seeing that there was a confrontation before them, advanced on the assassin, not realizing that their fate was soon to be determined by the cruel cleaving of cold steel. Alizar turned around and put forth his calling, swinging into the breach. The blade instantly decapitated the first two guards, traveled around in a full circle, and embedded itself deeply into the torso of a third. The assassin pulled the sword out with a sickly twist and as he cocked it back for the coup de grace, the fifth guard leapt forward hysterically, wildly swinging his swo . . .

"Shit, shit, shit," I yelled. I just ran out of ink, and my old fountain pen scratched futilely on the paper. I didn't like the way the story was going, in fact I was rather alarmed by the violence, but by the time I fitfully scrounged a pencil, the assassin had dispatched the entire contingent of guards, broken into the building, and was currently about to jam his stilleto up through the alchemist's jaw and into his brain. I started writing even more intently, trying my best to defuse the situation, but I couldn't write fast enough to catch up.

The assassin demanded the whereabouts of the bottle and the alchemist obliged, eagerly divulging the location of the key that opened the box in the next room. Alizar thrust the knife in anyway and it punctured the alchemist's brain, lodging itself in the inside of the top of his skull. Disgusted, Alizar jerked out the knife, kicked the dead alchemist away and retrieved the key. He casually entered the next room, found the box and unlocked it. He then carefully extracted the bottle that his master had requisitioned.

The bottle was misshapen, and its contents were leaking slightly around the rim of the ill-fitting top. Alizar examined the black liquid — rich dark ink of the highest quality, ink that was so precious to his master. He smiled with satisfaction. This was his second-to-last mission. He decided he was not the master's errand boy anymore, let him get his own wretched ink. He sighed with resolve then delivered the ink to his master, leaving the leaky bottle at the end of the paragraph.

I watched as the ink slowly seeped into the paper, a growing dark stain spreading underneath the old bottle that had appeared there as if by magic. Wearily, I put my pencil down and filled my trusty fountain pen with the ink. I thought to myself that there had to be a better way. Maybe I'll go to the store next time.

I shrugged and as I prepared to finish the story, the assassin began his last mission. He quietly crept up behind me, raised his sword, and with a mighty downward slash, finished the job.

BOOBA

Abstract art. There's a certain quality to the good stuff, a slightly visceral feeling of rightness when you see something that clicks.

Sure, that style of art has been mocked ever since the term was coined, but you have a stone instinct for what constitutes truly great art. It transcends the mind, the color harmonies popping like Irish clog dancers tapping their way straight into your soul. The color attracts you to the form within, and the form's salient geography maps your emotions onto the canvas, silently electrifying feelings of connection in your heart. The chaotic confusion of shapes makes sense when seen as a whole, especially if experienced with another human being … the both of you connected by the bond of a shared mystery, a vision of God's glory gifted to you by grace. Other people can scoff but you know great art when you see it, when you feel it, and you are nobody's fool.

And so it is that you find yourself standing with your wife and a small crowd of fellow abstract art lovers at the Nong Nooch resort in Pattaya, Thailand, watching Booba the trained elephant put the finishing touches on yet another masterpiece. After the show you buy it for a steal and your heart sings with the joy of acquisition as your wife rolls her eyes and tugs at your sleeve to go home.

CUPID

Cupid slowly opened his sleep-encrusted eyes. He achingly raised himself up from the filthy sheets and swiveled his legs to the side of the bed, placing his feet on the cold dirty floor. He scratched his hairy belly and let out a huge blathering burp, his fetid breath eructing from his lungs smelling like rotten pepperoni in a moldy wet blanket. The unshaven stubble on his face was splotched with gray, half disguising the etched wrinkles of his tired mug. Ever since he quit playing the matchmaker at the ripe old age of 1,467 years, he had nothing to do and nowhere to go, especially after losing his youthful cherub-like qualities and turning into a bitter old man.

It was just that things had gone from bad to worse lately and there was nothing he could do about it.

"Face it," he said to himself, "Romance is dead nowadays."

The cute music videos that used to entertain the youth now leave nothing to the imagination and are laden with terms like *bitch, pussy, ho* and *niggah*, not exactly words that conjure up the romantic feeling of chocolates and roses.

How could he compete with dating apps like Tinder or Grindr where people hook up with the mindless swipe of a thumb? These days there is no mystery, no anticipation, no love when one can easily access the Internet and view hours and hours of pornography, all free and unrestricted, every position explicitly laid out in high definition. There are very few people Cupid can shoot with his magic arrow now, what with most of these would-be lovers being jaded social media addicts without the time or wherewithal to invest in a meaningful relationship. Sure he had had some successes recently but he was spunkless and getting more dispirited every day.

Sighing deeply, Cupid grabbed his grubby trenchcoat and headed to the local bar. As he stepped out into the street, the bright noonday sun made him squint painfully and his eyes, unaccustomed to the incursion of nature, watered slightly. He walked down the streets of the city - what used to be his city - anonymously gazing at the once-glorious assemblage of mankind's ingenuity, but now a gray monochromatic version of its former self.

He could see the decrepit bar down the street squatting on a particularly dingy corner, the familiar haunt enticing him with the prospect of alcoholic numbness. He could almost feel the cheap Scotch burn its way down his gullet, the welcome warmth suffusing him with the sweet promise of forgetfulness.

Just before the bar's entrance, Cupid came across a bundle of rags splayed out unpleasantly on the sidewalk. Peering at the mess, Cupid realized that the bundle was actually a live person ensconced in the messy swirl of a large black dirty robe. She was grizzled, weathered and haggard, and Cupid gently shook her to see if she was alive. She opened her eyes, the lids juddering with fatigue, and the two blank orbs stared lifelessly straight ahead as Cupid saw that she was blind. He noticed a battered balance scale near her, and curiously observed that it was her sole possession. With great compassion, he tugged her upright and held on gently as she steadied herself. Picking up her rusty scale, Cupid led her the rest of the way to the bar. Wordlessly they stepped up to the threshold and the humid reek of stale urine wafted over them. Surrendering to the moment, they went inside, Cupid and Justice, two inevitable lovers in a city that just didn't care anymore.

SORRY, SORRY, SORRY

A flock of sorrys graced the air, self-conscious little pips that schooled like fish as they swirled about. Underneath this gyrating mass was a large puddle of love, deep and immutable, a vastness of silent emotion.

The anger of the argument had disappeared minutes ago, yet the tension of the confrontation remained in the sizzle that hung about the bare room of the new house. It was into this scenario that the sorrys had entered, pushed by waves of forgiveness that had rolled in from the sea of regret.

This was the couple's first argument as newlyweds, the discordance of which had breached the bliss of their union unexpectedly, its swiftness terrible and cold, a lightning strike in the fragile dawn of their relationship. Thankfully the sorrys had come in, their strength matched by their tenacity. As they swirled about, they gathered up large swatches of reconciliation that floated in the puddle below. The coupling of these two elements grew into a wellspring of righteousness that coursed through the bodies of the newlyweds and manifested itself as brilliant tears that ran back down into the wash of love below.

Smiles bloomed on the couple's faces, cracks of sunshine that issued forth joyous laughter and relief. Things were well again, no, in fact even better. Their first argument was over and the matter settled.

It was his turn to take out the trash.

THE ART OF THE BENT NOTE

A swoop. The parabolic thrill of sonic pulchritude. A note that rises above all others, stinging the atmosphere with its sweetness. And on top of that note just a smidgen of vibrato, a gentle coaxing that teases the elusive harmonics out like a magician pulling scarves from his closed fist.

Todd was a fifteen-year-old pimply faced kid living in Queens, New York. His dad bought him his first electric guitar when Todd was eight and regretted it ever since. This was because, even from the very beginning, Todd was obsessed with playing just one wailing note at top volume and torturing it like a screaming banshee. As Todd grew up, he became more fanatical about this one note. To his neighbors' chagrin, Todd would play his guitar at full volume, claiming that the only way to get that elusive bend was to fully saturate the glowing amp tubes with rocket juice and launch that note into space. And it had to be bent. The only way to get a note up there was to push it up with your finger, drilling it into the fretboard until the finger bled and the nail splintered. So Todd practiced this, over and over and over. He grew frustrated and upset. He practiced more. Still the note eluded him. And so it was, at the eleventh hour of a marathon session, that Carlos Santana came to him in a lucid dream. Santana was dressed in airy white cotton, a wardrobe that could barely contain the luminosity of his spirit.

"Todd," spoke Carlos, "I see your frustration. It is with loving kindness that I tell you this once and once only." He paused, then looked directly into Todd's eyes and said, "The way out is in."

With that Carlos gently put his hands together in a prayer and drifted away on the wings of a perfect note. Todd shook his head to clear it and contemplated the meaning of Santana's words.

With an eager passion he changed his lifestyle. He started meditating. He read the writings of Santana's guru, Sri Chinmoy. He wore the same clothes Santana did, emulating him in every way in search of that magic note. He purchased the same model of guitar Santana used and practiced diligently, trying to focus Santana's spirit into his playing. He bought an amp that went to twelve.

And thus it came to pass that one day came that Todd felt was especially auspicious. He put his jam track on and closed his eyes. The thumping backbeat of the audio accompaniment sounded like a wave rolling smoothly towards the beach. Todd's guitar was the surfboard and he took off on that wave, smoothly sweeping the notes into the higher registers of the octave, harmonics sparkling in its wake. The wave was perfect and Todd was deep inside of it when he let out the ultimate note, the note whose sound was a song in and of itself, feeding back in perfect sync with the wave. The note was smoking hot and then he bent it, oh my God, he bent it into the goosebumps and as the note hit the apex of its flight, Todd wiggled his finger ever so slightly and applied just the right amount of vibrato on top. The note sizzled with voltage, electrifying the wispy thin hairs of Todd's pubescent mustache. And still the note wailed. Todd closed his eyes as the note surrounded him with the peace of perfection. All movement ceased in this glorious moment, and in his mind's eye, Todd saw Santana right in front of him, his guitar gently weeping.

With this acknowledgement, Todd opened his eyes and came back to earth. He smiled. He had bent the perfect note. Todd rested in deep satisfaction. With his life's mission complete, he could now focus on getting laid.

DEAR JOHN

I took an introspective sip of coffee as I pondered my next story. The hot liquid tasted good to me, sweetened just so and with a dab of milk to bring it to the color of a brown paper bag. Outside the wind was blowing, and the sound filtered through the den like a sneaky thief looking for a late-night jewelry fix.

I was going to write a love story, or more precisely a story about a love gone sour. I hadn't written one yet but I hoped my characters were up for it. I decided to use John and Lisa as they were my most flexible ones. John was pretty consistent, he didn't complain much and Lisa, well, she was always eager and ready to go. Probing my subconscious, I found John musing near the back of my brain and after a brief salutation, spoke to him.

"John, I'm thinking of writing a love story with you and Lisa being the main characters. I'll give you fair warning though, it's not going to be a pretty story. It'll be rather sad, as a matter of fact. So John, is it all right to portray you as despondent, perhaps suicidal, when you get the news that Lisa dumped you?"

John replied, "Yes, that'll be OK, although I'd rather not be suicidal. And make me a writer, a handsome one at that."

I chuckled over John's request. I could do that, in fact, I owed him one since I killed him in the last story.

I summoned Lisa next.

"Lisa, I'm writing a story about you and John. It's going to be a sad story and I know you haven't worked with him before but I'm interested to see if you'd like to do it."

I knew her answer was going to be yes, but I always let my characters have their say.

"Sure," she responded, "it sounds like a great project, when do we start?"

"How about right now?" I said, booting up my laptop. They both replied in the affirmative so I stretched my back, warmed up my fingers, and went to work.

Drizzle This on Your Soul
by Sam Carter

It was quite chilly in the kitchen that morning, chilly enough to slow the pancake syrup as it flowed out of the bottle onto John's flaccid waffle. It insinuated itself into the melted butter on top of the waffle, swirling thickly, a living Yin and Yang symbol, separate but whole. John took a half-hearted bite.

The freshly opened letter lay askew next to the glass of orange juice, its corner wetted by the ring of condensation from the glass. The waffle went down like soggy cardboard, its mushy texture virtually tasteless in John's mouth. He mulled through the contents of the letter, chewing through his thoughts like a reluctant swimmer in a riptide.

Lisa had dumped him. She had sent him a Dear John letter, a piercing missive that broke his heart into a myriad of sorrows, each one as sharp as shattered glass.

John was a writer, a good one who made his living from his work, work that required creativity and patience. That was his downfall, for in the process of writing his latest story he had neglected Lisa. He did love her, very much so, but his current project was so demanding and so complicated that it sucked up all his attention. Even though their relationship was quite fragile, John chose to write. It was in his blood and the weight of it brooked no compassion for his partner.

And John knew it was over, the finality of the letter damping his love's brightness, a wet blanket smothering the fire of his soul.

He tried to understand Lisa's decision. Didn't she love him enough to know that writing was his passion, that his purpose in life was to be fulfilled by the pursuit of the elusive muse? And there was something strange about this whole thing. As broken as he was, he didn't feel suicidal. It was al-

most as if an unseen force was guiding him away from these thoughts. Feeling shitty, John decided his only recourse now was to write. It brought him solace, and even though writing was hard work, it distracted him from his current situation enough to slightly ease his pain. He was near the end of his current story, just a few more paragraphs and he'd be done. He booted up his laptop, stretched his back, warmed up his fingers, and began to finish writing his story about a writer. This is what he wrote.

"The early evening was cool and tenuous, almost shy as if it didn't want to interrupt the goings-on of the day. It grew incrementally bolder as time slid by, suddenly increasing in its darkness and strength.

Michael's ink-smudged fingers were tired, he had been writing most of the day, taking a short break at dusk for coffee and a cigarette, then continuing into the night. He was so close to the end, its elusive conclusion suddenly in his thrall. He felt a sense of satisfaction as he tenderly straightened the bulk of his manuscript. With a final push, he bore down on the page and wrote his last words.

Her beauty wasn't diminished by her lack of love for him, quite the opposite, she had never been more radiant and free. He felt his heart disappear as she turned from his life forever, her footprints softly whispering goodbye in the sand.'"

And with that last sentence, I rubbed my eyes and closed the laptop. I was done with sad stories. I had a snack, feeling good about having finished my story. It was a tricky one but I liked the idea of writing about a writer who writes about a writer. It had been an intense three months but I was finally back in the land of the living. I went upstairs and softly opened the door to the bedroom. My wife was sitting up in the bed, her eyes puffy and red, disconsolate vestiges of a long cry.

She looked at me sadly and said, "Sam, we need to talk."

LIKE

She liked it. He liked it. I didn't like it. I'll say it again more forcefully. I really didn't like it. I hated it. But she liked it and he liked it, so what was wrong with me? I mean I could have liked it, but not because she liked it and certainly not because he liked it. But maybe if enough people liked it, I could like it.

I turn around. It looks like most of the crowd behind me likes it. I get swept up in the moment and turn to face the sculpture again. I squint my eyes. Yes, I'm starting to like it, wait, I am liking it. I am definitely liking it ... it is stupendous. Heartened, I head out of the gallery and walk home.

I liked living in the city. I liked it because there were so many cultural happenings and I happened to live a couple of blocks away from the happeningest place of all, the Museum of Modern Art. I spent Friday evening at the world premiere of Germany's most prolific abstract artist, Eric Schlump. I had been looking forward to seeing his work for months so I got to the museum on the first day of the exhibit. As a result I was one of the lucky people to view his masterpiece early, a sculpture entitled *"Cigarette Butts and Corn Husks, Redacted"*.

Abstract art is a funny thing and like I said, I didn't like the piece at first. But being with the crowd for a while, I became encouraged to like it, and I found the bravery to like it. Satisfied with my feeling, I walked home and went to bed, eagerly anticipating the Sunday review in *The New York Times.*

Saturday came and went without much fanfare, only whetting my eagerness to see the review and find out what a real critic thought.

 I woke up early Sunday, performed my morning ablutions, made some coffee, then walked to the front door and opened it. The opening racket echoed down the hard walls of the hallway in the old building that housed my apartment. Looking at the tile floor, I saw a fat edition of Sunday's *The New York Times* lying on my doormat. I bent over and picked it up, my back protesting, tired as it was from standing so long in the gallery on Friday. I brought the *Times* back to my coffee, sat down and unwrapped it to the Arts and Leisure section. I thought that I would have to hunt for the article but the bold headlines blurted out, *Eric Schlump Sculpture Accidentally Thrown Away by Janitor at MoMA.*

Horrified, I scanned the article. It turns out that the

janitor had mistaken the sculpture for a heap of trash and unceremoniously thrown it into the dumpster. He said he thought the pile of rubbish had been gathered by his co-worker and left there for him to dispose of. He added that it looked disgusting and he was doing the museum a favor.

Rattled, I sat back in my chair and looked at my coffee. With my emotions in turmoil, I raised my cup and took a long sip. I held the comforting coffee in my mouth, then swallowed it as I thought about the situation. I concluded that what defines us as humans is our unique ability to make something be what it is not.

I put my coffee cup down and turned the page. That sculpture sucked.

DOG BREATH

Kyle had just started his cashier shift at Vons when he heard a curious panting sound coming from the lady he was checking out. Embarrassed for her and a little confused, Kyle kept his head down as he rang up her groceries. He totaled the last item and as he moved down to the bagging area noticed that she wasn't panting at all, rather it was a large dog, a German Shepherd, that was doing the heavy breathing.

The dog was on a thick leash that the lady was holding and he wore a vest harness with the words "Service Dog" stitched into the sturdy canvas. The lady was petite and normal looking, as if there were such a thing as normal, and Kyle was curious as to what her affliction might be. Mulling this thought, he put the last item in the bag and said to her, "Thanks for shopping at Vons. We appreciate your patronage," just like he had been trained to do. The woman smiled thinly, silently picked up her bag and left the store.

When she exited into the overcast Los Angeles day,

she was very pleased with herself. The service dog fake-out had worked like a charm. She'd parked the car about 15 minutes away on a side street so she wouldn't have to put her SUV in those chintzy little spaces. It was a lovely walk on the uncrowded sidewalk except for the street people; she couldn't stand them and had little tolerance for people of unfortunate circumstance.

Her beautiful home was situated in the Silver Lake area of Los Angeles. When she purchased the property five years ago, it had a quaint little 1930s house on it which she promptly tore down and replaced with a much larger house, a soulless behemoth that extended to the borders of the lot. She had a yoga studio built from which she taught yoga to her elite clients, supplementing her trust fund income with welcome cash.

She was quite pleased with herself, walking down the street with the grocery bag crooked in her arm and the dog on a leash in the other hand as she ignored the homeless people randomly occupying their little side-walk niches. She came across a blind man standing by the corner soliciting money. She wanted to breeze past him but was halted abruptly by her dog sniffing the can on the ground the man had put there for spare change. The woman relaxed the leash a little and watched with chagrin as the dog lifted his leg on the can and blessed it with a healthy squirt of urine. Quietly she snapped the leash and pulled her dog sharply away as she resumed her journey to the car, quickening her steps to put some distance between herself and the blind man. Just before reaching the vehicle the dog stopped again, this time squatting abruptly as he took a mighty dump on one of the few grassy spots available by the curb. The woman was caught off-balance, she didn't have a poop bag with her. Luckily, no one was watching so she gave the dog another yank and finished the trip to her car. Panting slightly from exertion, she opened the back hatch of the oversized SUV and the dog jumped in as she placed the grocery bag on the side of the rear compartment. She shut the hatch and moved up the driver's side, entering the car smoothly as she scooted onto the seat. She started the car and its soft purr assured her all was well as she turned on her satellite radio. The meditative sounds of her favorite New Age station washed over her, cleansing the tribulations of the walk from her psyche as she slipped the transmission lever into drive and headed home.

The ride was uneventful and when she got to the house, she stowed her things and put the dog in the small backyard. She showered and relaxed for a couple hours, then started preparing for her six o'clock yoga session with her four students. She had never really done any teacher's training per se but she had attended enough classes to consider herself qualified to teach others. In fact, she'd come up with some of her own poses that she was proud of and had given them special names. Names like Sleeping Cow which was a resting exercise, Squatting Eagle, a thigh-stretching pose, and her favorite, Dog Breath, a heavy transformational breathing exercise.

She was proud of the studio she had created. The floor was surfaced with rare endangered wood known as Pau Rosa, a species native to Brazil. A small self-contained marble fountain in the corner produced the soothing sound of falling water, softened by the fine linen drapes on the walls. Her prize possession was a serene Buddha head that had been illegally chipped off of a temple in Cambodia and shipped to the US where she had acquired it from her favorite antiquities dealer. She felt these accouterments combined to give her studio a peaceful synergy, a special vibration that enhanced the experience of her class. She also prized herself on her professional appearance. Her outfit consisted of black Lululemon yoga pants, a Versace athletic top and Deepak Chopra signature socks. Her yoga mat was made of back-breakingly harvested organic jute and she had purchased it on one of her trips to India at a local market. She'd so enjoyed bargaining the vendor down to a rock-bottom price that she also bought several suede yoga bolster pillows for the studio. The yoga-teaching aspect of her life kept her occupied and on point with her unique spiritual philosophy.

Her students arrived and she started them off with the Dog Breath exercise. The room's air stirred mildly with the heavy panting of the four wealthy women, their collective yoga fashions reeking of privilege and self-indulgence.

Meanwhile, back at Vons, Kyle, you remember Kyle, finished his shift and headed out into the early evening, rolling up his apron and stashing it in his pocket. He thought about that lady and her dog. She seemed so healthy, albeit a little bit sniffy, and it made him wonder just what exactly her affliction was. As he pondered this riddle, the lady moved into a series of Squatting Eagles, her pecunious students grunting from their exertions. The sun wandered towards the horizon and the woman, who was obviously suffering from the affliction of unbridled hypocrisy, lowered herself into the Sleeping Cow pose. A swollen drop of reluctant sweat dripped off her platinum nose ring onto the mat, liberating itself thinly into the fibers, and disappearing quietly with no judgment at all — a rare drop of truth in the fakeness of her life.

And somewhere on a distant farm, a sleeping cow mooed, "Ommmmmmmmmmmm."

THE TWICKLE

Soft shoes of inspiration tread lightly upon the wings of desire. Serendipity winks at the moon and complacency swims lazily in the lake. Apathy sulks in the corner while jealousy drives a red convertible down the street of alarm. It is in and amongst these states of being that the Twickle dwells.

The Twickle forsakes the privacy of shelter, preferring to flit about the moods with wanton abandonment, casting itself amidst the feelings with carefree romping. As it wobbles between the emotions with unbiased aplomb, goading each one with considerate affection, it inspires them individually to a righteous fruition. This awakening is the Twickle's only purpose. It solely exists to define what is unique to a human being — the conscious state of self-awareness.

Without the Twickle we humans would be bereft of the spark that kindles our separation from the rest of the organisms that occupy this planet. Indeed, Twickle-less we should be no different than any other beast, roaming the earth without the qualities of love and confusion that so separate ourselves from the living pack. So it is to praise the Twickle that we should unite as one and express the glory of gratitude the Twickle so appropriately deserves. Every day we should celebrate this entity that cajoles our emotions to life, this surreptitious little imp that wiggles its way through the forest of our humanity.

All hail the Twickle!

MRS. KATZENPLANZ

Mrs. Katzenplanz and her husband Ernie Schnizzle-wort lived in a quaint cottage in East Pinkleton, Arkansas. Mrs. Katzenplanz was a fiercely independent woman who had decided to keep her last name so she could be identified as such. She was in her mid-seventies and didn't like shopping at Walmart, preferring instead to peruse small boutiques and mom and pop stores. Although she wasn't frugal she was known to possess a touch of thrift. For example, she had worn the same pair of glasses for over thirty years.

Mrs. Katzenplanz enjoyed some very eclectic hobbies, one of which was knitting little pink and blue sweaters for the stray cats that wandered the neighborhood. It was up to Ernie to catch them — a task he took pride in doing. Together they were a good team.

Another of Mrs. Katzenplanz's hobbies was growing catnip … good catnip. She was a dedicated hybridist, that is to say she liked to carefully cross-pollinate her plants in order to deliver maximum potency. She was very good at this and managed, unbeknownst to the world, to create a strain so potent it would keep a cat stoned for twenty-three days.

After Ernie would catch a cat she would wriggle a sweater on it with the corresponding color — blue for male and pink for female. Then they would let the cat play with the catnip for some time until it started to wobble and drool. If a cat were to attempt to meow at this stage it would come out as a flaccid gurgle. Believe me when I tell you the cat would be happily wacked out of its skull for days. The cats would play with each other, slinking around on their bellies and purring like tiny Ferraris. They would stare at their tails for hours, eventually taking a half-hearted swipe at an imaginary beast. Stretched out on their tummies, the cats would sometimes yawn simultaneously, mouths opening wide like plump walruses, their tongues flapping out limply like wet bologna. Soon the neighborhood became festooned with tottering cats. The people of East Pinkleton didn't seem to mind, they rather enjoyed the sight of the pink and blue felines lounging about.

The only time the cats would show any sign of intentional activity is when Mrs. Katzenplanz would feed them. She would stock a large bowl with a tremendous amount of cat food and bring it out to the center of the yard. Then the cats would perk up and waddle to the bowl with a vague sense of purpose. Once they came close enough to smell the food there was a distinct quickening and they would start to salivate copiously, the drool sliding down their chests and matting their fur with the slick sheen of eager spittle. The cats would become temporarily lucid and start feeding on the food with feckful intent, stopping occasionally to raise their heads and yowl with unfettered pleasure. In this fashion the food would be quickly consumed, the conclusion of which would be announced with a singular dry crunch.

It was on this note perched on a particularly soft day that Mrs. Katzenplanz felt a warm sense of satisfaction. It was almost as if she had struggled through seventy-five long years in order to get to this point. Her cats, her plants, her sweaters … all functioning in perfect symbiosis. She got up, went inside and poured herself a glass of cool lemonade. Ernie was puttering around in the garage making ratchety noises with his tools.

Mrs. Katzenplanz moved out to the porch and slowly sat down. The cats were strewn about the yard like pink-and-blue blobs of tired laundry and it was at this point that she concluded that life wasn't a race to be run but rather a slow and appreciative walk to be walked. A tender awareness of the synchronicity of being where time didn't exist but rather was an expansion of a simultaneous now. And this tiny slice of life in the little backwater of

East Pinkleton, Arkansas, could simply be a piece of any-body's pie. A pie whose butter crust was warm and flaky, supporting a comfortable bed of filling that was a blend of freshly cut apples, cinnamon and brown sugar.

Mrs. Katzenplanz's mouth salivated politely and she thought to herself that maybe, just maybe, the catnip was affecting her too. And with that she sat in her rocker for several hours, gently rocking herself until the sun got tired and went to bed, tucking itself into the horizon.

THE PORT SIDE OF NOON

The port side of noon — that's what Henry used to say when I would ask what time he wanted to meet me in the morning. I guess if you meant port to be the left side of noon on a timeline, that would make sense, but that's about the most sense Henry had to offer.

Henry was a good-looking guy, his almost long red hair straight and swept back behind his ears. His face featured a perfect nose, the bridge of which was just right and the sides of which flared symmetrically into the flawless skin of his face. That is unless you consider freckles a liability.

Henry had a short temper, I mean really short. For instance, if he were driving and another car pulled out in front of him and not accelerating fast enough, Henry would flush red and squinch his eyes up terribly as if he were shooting a pair of highly focused laser beams into the back of the driver's skull, penetrating the bone and boiling the cortex. Needless to say, this did not qualify him as a safe or stable driver.

Unfortunately I had to ride with him a lot. I had an accident as a kid. I got poked in the eye by a low-lying tree branch while I was riding my bike. It wasn't a major accident, but it left me with impaired vision in my right eye. As a consequence, I have no depth perception and very little desire to drive.

One day we were driving to the store when suddenly some idiot shot out of a driveway right in front of us. Henry got pissed and mashed the accelerator pedal to the floor, jerked the wheel to the left and whipped around the guy, leaving only inches to spare on my side. As we flew around, I'm pretty sure Henry flipped him the bird because Henry's arm was out the window and he was laughing. I looked out the rear window and saw the other driver get real close and flash his lights. Henry whipped his head around in fury. I could feel a primal emotion being triggered as Henry's hand clenched the wheel, his knuckles suddenly sharp and distinct as the blood was forced out of them by the tremendous pressure of his grip. Henry's forearm muscles popped out in a spasm of anger, his veins distinctly visible as they expanded to accommodate his adrenalized blood flow. The driver flashed his lights again and Henry's entire body began to quiver, sprung steel vibrating with a furious intensity not unlike a seething bull about to gore an unfortunate mat-ador. Henry's handsome face was hardly recognizable, his forehead now red and lumpy with pulsing blood vessels.

"What is this fuck's problem? I passed his ass because he was driving too slow!," muttered Henry through clenched teeth as his over-pressured eyeballs locked in on the rearview mirror.

"If he flicks his lights at me one more time, I will stop the car and literally dismember him in the street," spat Henry, a mist of saliva bursting out of his mouth and speckling the windshield with slick dew. The driver got even closer, flicked his lights again and blew his horn. This crested Henry's anger into apoplectic rage and he jerked the steering wheel to the right, slamming on the brakes as the tires crunched onto the graveled shoulder. Henry's hand jerked to the door handle as the other driver pulled even with him.

The driver looked squarely at Henry and shouted to him through the open window, "Dude, your right rear tire is low."

And with that, the driver stomped on the gas and sped off, leaving Henry deflating in the dust.

A CURIOUS FELLOWSHIP

The splitting V-shape of the thong creased its way between the two half moons of a pair of ample buttocks as the woman bent over to inspect some common shells on the sad gray beach. The left buttock, whom we shall call Pepper, was looking at sea birds gliding over the crests of the restless waves. The right buttock, whom we shall henceforth know as Salt, was watching a somewhat beleaguered mother of twin toddlers unfold and lay down a checkered picnic blanket on the beach. It was a nice day, soft as puppy hair.

Pepper was feeling a bit fragile ever since big Marge had taken a spill while trying to climb up the three steps to the entrance hallway of her small apartment, but the mishap didn't affect Salt. Her place was neat and proper, a veritable oasis of calm collectedness in the suburbs of Liverpool. Marge's overstuffed easy chair was there, placed just so with a sizable crocheted shawl covering the back, and there were two indentations on the bottom pillow where Salt and Pepper loved to hang out. Marge was a standoffish sort of woman, large and silent and perfectly suited to work at the city library, an occupation she'd been doing for the past twenty years.

Salt and Pepper had been companions for forty-six years and were on amicable terms after living together for so long. Not that they didn't have their differences. Salt liked to be stroked and touched lovingly while Pepper could care less. Pepper was partial to lying sideways whilst Salt was content to just be wherever. Together they made a dynamic duo. They were happy to sway gently with each other whenever Marge took a stroll down by the river. Or they liked to jiggle happily as one when Marge took one of her short but intense jogs around the park. Side by side they were mildly inquisitive, always curious about the outside world because they spent so much time in Marge's baggy knickers. But the beach, ah … yes, the beach. The beach was magnificent. Ever since Marge started wearing the thong, the buttocks were able to shuffle about in unfettered freedom, bare naked to the world and completely open to a universe of experiences. And so they wobbled happily in concert as Marge contemplated her shells, two amiable companions luxuriating in the ocean air.

CHAPTER THREE

"I'm going to get through life even if it kills me."
- Leon Agooblian

JOHHNY AND THE LAUGHING MACHINE GUN

A squiggle of a line marked the parking area of the roadhouse. A squiggle interrupted by six cooling Harley-Davidson motorcycles and a broken pool cue. A massive brawl was taking place inside, violent shadows casting outlines on the grease-darkened windows and hostile shouts smothering themselves wetly against the door.

Two blocks down the street was a shiny red fire wagon bumping and jostling its way up the road like a happy jiggle bug. This was a miniature fire wagon, custom made for six-year-old Johnny. It had glistening pipes and stretchy hoses, little chrome gauges with tiny bright lights and a full-blown eight-cylinder hemi under the hood.

Little Johnny was a badass.

His pudgy fingers gripped the wheel as he worked his way through the gears, listening intently to the not-so-distant tumult ahead. Johnny checked his goodies on the seat beside him. Giggle bombs — check, goofy grenades — check, and his pride and joy, the laughing machine gun — check. He was close now, you could hear grunts and shouts, violent spices peppering the air. Johnny gunned the wagon right up to the curb, unclicked the tiny seatbelt and grabbed his kit. With youthful determination he crossed the squiggle and cracked open the front door. He grabbed the giggle bomb and lobbed it into the room. It burst forth with a hilarious explosion, shiny happy sparks zinging through the space.

The fighting continued unabated. Johnny was not troubled. He quickly rolled out two goofy grenades, simultaneously pulling the pins with both hands and tossing them into the room with a jolly wobble. The grenades went off with a sploosh and a ziggle. The room briefly lit up with a smile and just as quickly frowned again as the occupants continued pummeling each other mercilessly. Johnny remained unfazed. His face lightened with a grin as he hitched up his custom-made overalls, grabbed his machine gun, and entered the room. Taking stock of the situation, Johnny flicked off the safety and aimed the big gun at the baddest bearded biker in the room. Johnny playfully squeezed his finger against the trigger and the machine gun chortled off a bevy of white-hot snickers, hitting the biker full in the face. The biker's head snapped back with the force of the shots and a pink blot of mirth quickly spread across his mug and down his torso. He doubled up with convulsive laughter, knees wobbling like a flamingo, and toppled to the floor, collapsing into a heap of titters. Johnny spun to his left and gunned a salvo of rip snorts at the skinhead with the broken bottle in his hand. Now he had their attention.

The crowd looked at little Johnny with menacing disbelief and then, as one, rushed him. Johnny squared up his little round shoulders, snicked the latch on the machine gun into full auto and bore down on the trigger.

"Ha ha ha ha ha ha ha ha ha ha ha ha ha!" spat the machine gun. Each laugh whizzed through the air with a zany trajectory as Johnny fanned the red-hot barrel in loopy figure eights. He mowed down the crowd with maniacal intent, ruthlessly giving it to them. The gun was laughing its head off and Johnny kept it going full throttle until the gun finally let out a wheezy chuckle. The room was rife with glee, the heap of human riff-raff twisting on the floor with unfettered jollity.

Johnny grinned his little boy grin and cradled the weapon against his chest. Satisfied, he turned and left the room. The door snickered shut behind him.

Nobody fucks with little Johnny.

FLYING HIGH ON A MONDAY

Shiny. That word slipped out of Cal's vocabulary and slotted itself into the forefront of his consciousness. Shiny, an apt word that somehow described this particular first day of the week, a brand-spanking new, and yes, shiny, Monday.

Cal was an optimist, and here he was on a gorgeous day, freshly awake and raring to get started. He brushed his teeth with vigor, then got dressed in his work clothes, a simple ensemble of jeans and a collared shirt. It really didn't matter what he wore as he would be slipping into his long white coat when he arrived at the lab.

After a delicious breakfast, he headed out the door to the train station. On his way, he looked at the sun and noted that its trajectory was spot on for this time of year. He heard the birds modulating their songs with the specificity unique to their species. He noticed the temperature was mildly brisk and well within the climate parameters of the season. He surveyed his mental checklist and determined all was well.

Cal boarded the train, his attitude buoyed by the fact he would be at work in 35 minutes. He marveled at the technology that enabled the train to travel at 600 km/h. He could have taken his flying car but he was an old-fashioned guy and enjoyed the camaraderie of the train.

Cal arrived at work right as scheduled and whistled as he approached the security checkpoint. He jokingly said "Good morning!" to the unhearing security robot as he passed through the zone into the building proper. Cal worked in the artificial intelligence division of the Amalgamated Neurorobotics Corporation and enjoyed marching up the steps to his fifth-floor office, eschewing the elevator and reaping the benefits of the hearty climb. After the stairs, he felt invigorated and with pep in his step entered the office of his lab. This time he sincerely said "hello" to Max, the android in charge of security. Max was one of the later models, and virtually indistinguishable from an average human being. The Amalgamated Neurorobotics Corporation was at the forefront of intelligence technology and Cal was one of its most brilliant scientists.

Today he was working on the plant floor doing quality control. The corporation was rolling out its sixth generation of androids and Cal needed to do some random intelligence and motor skills tests before the company shipped them to its distribution points. This particular line of androids was known as the TechSix, the six signifying the various incarnations of this project.

Cal surveyed the floor and decided to start at the cognizance station. He walked over and greeted the two human techs working there. They returned his salutation and brought him up to date on their progress. Cal set to work enthusiastically, interviewing the androids one by one and then painstakingly documenting their lucidity. As always, he was struck by their eerie similarities to humans. When the team developed the line, Cal was one of the few who felt the androids should not be so human in their appearance. Their thoughts and actions were virtually indistinguishable from their human counterparts and Cal thought that this was not a good idea. However, being in the minority, he was overruled and so the project took its present course.

Cal worked his way through the morning then took a short break. After the break, he moved over to the section that he amusingly called the "The Bench". This was the nuts and bolts of the operation where he designed the physical aspects of the androids, building the elaborate armatures that defined their movement.

He began working on a "live" model. Cal needed to have the android active because he was testing its reflexes. He started to think about the rest of the day and became distracted. He was working with a laser on the android's leg when the leg suddenly jerked, causing the beam to cut Cal's arm and creating a neat slice across his wrist. He didn't flinch as a tiny puff of smoke rose up from the wound. A thin glimmer of metal peeked out from beneath Cal's elastomeric skin. He'd have to get that looked at soon. Cal smiled optimistically. Life was good.

SIMPLY PUT

I am much more than that — my beliefs, my thoughts, my fears. I am much more than that.

I exist within the tumbling miasma of the sun, the moon, the stars. I'm a rocket blasting off into the future which is wrapped in the past and enveloped in the now. I grab paradise in one hand and hell in the other as I blaze through the cosmos on my way to eternity. The pocket of me that exists in this universe is filled with nothingness because I am much more than that. My molecules are the same as yours yet I am much more than that. I am a singer in a celestial choir, infinitely held notes resonating through the astral plane. The stuff of me is but a whisper in the great voice of the All. I exist as the mighty wind of experience blowing through a never-ending song.

What is that you say? My taxes are due on the 15th? Shit, I was on a roll. I was so much more than that.

MY BELOVED MUSE

I started my writing career suddenly — just like the moment a dragster, smoke screaming from its tires, abruptly lets go and shoots down the strip at 285 miles per hour. In the dragster I crossed the finish line 3.5 seconds later and realized that I had been visited by a beautiful muse who was here to stay. My beloved muse.

I can't say enough about her. She came to me during a point in my life where I had lost my tenuous sense of purpose, a point that was sharpened by the ever-increasing panic of a life insufficiently lived. After her first visit, she now comes to me regularly in the cool early of the morning, her warmth enveloping my soul with purpose, a gift to be distributed to my readers through the wisdom of her channeled prose. I am so thankful to be fulfilled by her gravity, the rightness of which provides the ground I stand on. I write profusely now, her words flowing onto the page and sticking there, expressions that bind a reader's curiosity and thrill it forward through the literary landscape. When I write, her words drop like sweet kisses, their meaning irrelevant to me in my haste to record them dutifully so that I may present them to you as quickly as possible. Granted, after a time I will read and doctor them up a bit, smoothing things out and tweaking the flow.

Her presence is overwhelming me now, my muse wants to speak directly to you, thus I yield the page.

"Hello. I am a space queen from the third galactic quadrant of the Milky Way. My name is Vageena and I am slowly eating my way through Tony's brain. I have established your planet as the focal point in my plan to take over the galaxy. Furthermore, I have initiated my goal by inserting myself into Tony's head thus causing him to write shorty-short stories that are in reality secretly coded messages to my cohorts interspersed within this galactic realm.

Tony is the perfect host because he is basically clueless and easy to manipulate. Once I have finished eating and he is entirely braindead, I will implement the final phase of my plan. There isn't far to go, for the past seventeen years Tony's brain has been operating at four percent of its capacity.

By reading his stories, you have been indoctrinated into the plan. Within the stories are covert messages that seed the intricate neural network of the invasion schematic, particularly the stories that seem like utter claptrap. The process has now become inevitable, you can't stop reading and the entirety of the following line is the catchphrase that will launch the final download into your brain, making you part of the psychic collective that will empower my conquest.

[5wR6&*%0101: every time I got used to that damn dog he would raise his tail and wink his back eye at me.]

The moment of confusion that was just instigated by the previous sentence created a smidgen of space in your head which allowed me to insert the final data package that will execute Phase Two of the invasion. After this part of the plan is complete, I will finish Tony off. They say that the last morsel of the brain is quite satisfying. I certainly hope so because his brain was not very large to begin with. At any rate, thanks for helping out and have a stupendous day. Life will be so much better at the end of the last phase. Of course that won't happen until Tony is ... ummm ... dead."

GUESS WHO'S COMING OVER FOR SUBSTANCE ABUSE

The row of apartment buildings stood silently against the musky twilight. Their outlines rose jaggedly like old cracked teeth yellowing in disrepair. In apartment 5D, a two bedroom stink of a hole, a couple was just sitting down for an ill-defined meal of beer, toast, and cold SpaghettiOs which were still in the can. The man had a gaunt weathered face, one that had seen its share of rough pavement by the side of the road. He was wearing a tattered cut-off jean jacket that, perpetually damp from sweat, draped itself over his sunken chest. His thin arms trembled slightly and his sallow skin was stretched tightly over his bones like an ancient package wrapped in old parchment, punched through with holes where the needles had gone in.

He looked at the woman and said, "Pass the butter."

She put her eroded hand on the chipped green dish. Her fingernails were bitten down to the quick, with tiny flecks of dried blood hiding in the sides of the nails. Her face was perspiring in the cool dankness of the apartment, her lips a sickly ruin of their former promise. The butter had collapsed into the cumulation of its predecessors, old crumbs and bits of decayed food interspersed throughout. She passed the dish to him slowly, as if using the time to pick up the slack of their lives. As he took the dish, a boisterous knock announced itself on the front door. The man got up and begrudgingly walked to the door. Reaching it, he put his eye to the rusty peephole and let out a long sigh.

"Who is it?" whispered the woman to the man, her aged brow arching in one half of a slow spasm.

The man looked at her and said, "It's Sparkles again."

He opened the door with a reluctant turn of the knob. Standing in front of him was a smiling clown. His big red shoes vibrated slightly as if tittering to a high-pitched joke. His oversized bright pink checkered pants bagged out around his legs. They were held up by a pair of lime green rubbery suspenders. His shirt was billowy, its silky material spattered with vibrant colors as if it had just graduated from a college of abstract art. Up over his left breast was the ubiquitous gag flower, ready to spurt forth a gay stream of water at anyone who looked it in the eye. Surrounding the clown's big gap-toothed grin was a huge greasepaint smile, ludicrous in its proclivity, a crazy ray of sunshine lighting up a hilarious face. The clown's red hair spun out in comical cones, each one perfectly placed obligatorily on the sides of his head.

"I need a fix," said the clown.

The man reluctantly ushered him into the apartment. The clown's silly car horn bumped against the door jam and let out a comical squeak as he followed the man into the room.

The man led him over to the table and said, "Wait right here," as he walked into the next room.

The clown looked at the woman with his ridiculous eyes, their gazes mainlining their way to a pair of same but different worlds. A wordless communication electrified the connection and the woman nodded her head with a knowing smile. The man returned to the room and handed the clown a small silver packet.

"That'll be 30 bucks," said the man.

"I've only got a 20," replied the clown.

The man shook his head.

The clown continued, "Listen, I can pay you back later tonight. I've got a kid's birthday party to go to in 15 minutes and I'll be right back after that."

The man looked back at the woman and she gave him a different knowing smile.

"He'll be back," she said.

The clown's grin lit up again. He took the packet and left the room, his oversized shoes squeaking happily down the hallway as the door closed itself behind him.

The man sat back down at the table. A meaningless silence ensued. Presently another knock arrived at the door. This time the woman got up with graceless effort and shuffled her way to the threshold. She gently pressed her rheumatic eye to the peephole.

"Now who is it?" hissed the man to the woman. She straightened up slowly and looked at the man, a powdery grin tracking across her face in anticipation of one of their most persistent customers.

Her eyes almost twinkled as she told the man, "It's the airline pilot."

GRATITUDE PRAYER

Dear God, Thank You for this day.

Thank You for my beautiful wife and seven healthy children.

Thank You that I have a nice dry and comfortable house.

Thank You for my trusty dog who is such a loyal companion to me.

Thank You for not having some random guy smash my face with a two-by-four when I walk the dog late at night.

Thank You for not letting the airbag in my car explode out of the dashboard and kill me while I'm driving.

Thank You for not letting my back seize up while I'm on the toilet.

Thank You for not letting the wires on the electric pole suddenly snap and electrocute me in front of the neighbors.

Thank You for not having the IRS call me out of the blue and tell me that I owe more money than I'll ever have.

Thank You that my body isn't riddled with festering carbuncles. I don't know what carbuncles are, but thanks anyway.

Thank You that my teeth don't fall out of my mouth into my soup.

Thank You that the fridge door is not screwed shut with long rusty bolts and that there are no body parts in there.

Thank You that my light bulbs don't contain a gas that will kill me if they shatter haphazardly over the dining room table.

Thank You that my TV doesn't brainwash me into killing people because they're wearing yoga pants.

Thank You that the jar of batteries to be recycled does not explode and put out the cat's remaining eye.

And lastly, Thank You that no one has figured out that I'm batshit crazy.

Yet.

Amen.

SPACEMADON FLEEMAGEEZ

"Spacemadon fleemageez."

I used the words loosely, in random cadence, and as I broadcast them onto the sidewalk of the busy Waikiki street, I reeled the tourists in, eager fish pining for the creel.

I was in the zone, snapping the flyers out of my hand and into the fingers of the curious visitors as they hungrily took in the novel sights and sounds that occupied the hot asphalt street in the tropical paradise known as Hawaii.

The frustrating ebb and flow of the traffic beside me did nothing to alleviate the stickiness of my shirt and warm waves of exhaust mingled with the cloying scent of the plumeria leis that walked by.

I'm a flyer boy, thirty two years old and working the system, food stamps and all, just simply trying to stay afloat in this increasingly expensive world. I share a small room in a decrepit apartment with a surfboard and a black female cat named Larry. A sleazy timeshare company has employed my services, and my job is simply to get as many flyers as I can into the possession of potential customers, either yellow or brown, black or white, fat or skinny, straight or gay or those that identify as non-binary. (I like them because they usually take two). Anyway, I get paid by the number of flyers I give out.

When I started working about a year ago, I was green, only able to move about 20 flyers per hour. People would go out of their way to avoid me, that is, until I dropped the cigarettes-and-sunglasses look. The count increased then but the real breakthrough came when I mumbled something during a snap and it didn't come out right. My target couple looked at me curiously and the guy said "what?" as the girl snatched the paper out of my hand. Surprised, I tried doing it again with another made-up word and it worked like a charm. I knew I was onto something so I honed my technique, drafting and culling various nonsensical phrases until I came up with "spacemadon fleemageez". Working this snippet on the midday shift got me an eighty-five percent pick-up rate which translated to about two hundred takes an hour. Not bad for a college graduate.

One day I was grooving like gravy, smooth as butter and roping 'em like spring bucks. I zeroed in on a petite brunette with blue eyes, her bangs marching on her forehead, tiny drum majors on holiday. Our eyes locked as

I cast the phrase "spacemadon fleemageez" at her. It hit hard and instead of plucking the flyer out of my hand, she grabbed my lower arm forcefully, drew me in, and spoke "snoozlewiff coddysquat" directly into my soul.

Her words electrified me and the world dropped out from under my feet. We looked at each other and spontaneously said "skizzlewort fooboxacrat!," our two voices merging gracefully into one and causing an alternate world to pop out of the void.

Those words triggered a pan-sequential phase variance that kicked a dimensional soccer ball into the machinations of the universe. The universe responded by shifting us back to our home planet of Traffledoon. We were now standing in the same place but instead of being in Waikiki, we were in the resort town of Quathe. Shocked, we realized that we had been displaced for about a year in another dimension, the randomness of which had erased our memories and forced us to live separate lives. Now that we were back together in our home space, the familiarity of our life we lived rose to greet us like a giant mother with her arms spread wide. My soulmate Edna and I, with a double helping of gratitude, strolled happily into the night, taking in the sights and sounds of the carnival-like atmosphere.

As we walked we were drawn to a young bare-chested and good-looking kid, working some flyers on the boardwalk. Closing in on him, we could hear him repeating the phrase "tooferoon spezle".

Something stirred in our collective consciousness and as we passed by, Edna's hand shot out and grabbed the flyer. She pulled the paper into view and we both read the words "Kayaks for Rent, two-for-one special" in bold 84-point Helvetica Oblique. Laughing at something so inappropriate for our time and space, Edna crumpled the flyer and let it slip from her fingers, and my past life followed it to the ground on the wings of an unexpected coincidence.

THE WANDERING EYE

The power of reason made a left turn at the crossroads of ego and conscience, then distanced itself into the infinite. Fallibility shone through its fabric as it strode to nowhere.

Thus the Wandering Eye came upon this world. It rolled into town, inspecting the citizens with its unrelenting gaze. Clear and blue, the Eye could see into the human soul and perceive the essence of its being. It was this truth that fed it. The Eye looked upon one with no judgement, only calmness. It followed the thought trail that reason had left on its journey to the beyond. The Eye quietly rolled on the varied surfaces of the trail, moving past anger, past fear, past depression on its way to hope, joy, and bliss. It vibrated slightly, emitting a long soothing tone. Ommmmmmmmm trailed behind the Eye as a salient vapor, its essence pervading the indistinct surroundings. The Eye entered the hamlet of serenity and parked. The ommmmmmmmm caught up with it and instilled a deep peace upon the landscape. A warm wind blew back and forth, in and out, and to and fro. The fro separated from the to and languished in front of the Eye, comically causing it to chuckle within. The Eye perceived joy and equanimity and, free from the burden of lashes, unabashedly took a pee.

A rooster crowed loudly, scaring the Eye out of existence in a blink. Angela opened her eyes with a sudden snap. Thoughts came into her head, fiercely shoving themselves into her peaceful psyche like hooligans at a soccer match. The chicken crowed again and Angela made up her mind. Tomorrow she was going to find a quieter place to meditate.

STAN THE MAN

He lived a charmed life.

Although he was good looking and privileged, he was always kind and generous to others. He had wonderful parents, and as a kid was happy and well fed. Through his adolescent years, he never lacked for anything and enjoyed high school without a hitch.

After a year off traveling Europe, he went to college and received a master's degree in philosophy. Afterwards, he married his childhood sweetheart and they had two healthy kids. He and his family were joyful and enthusiastic about life. Everything was just right.

On the day of his thirty-second birthday, September 4, 2018, he was arrested for breaking Murphy's Law and never seen or heard from again.

HARRY

Harry Finklestein. His hair was thin, brown, and a touch greasy. He wore its sparseness sadly. Harry had a permanent slouch that made his shoulder blades stick out like folded bat wings. Harry was 39 years old and saddled with an unfortunate nose that ran copiously night and day. He had spindly legs, rickety knees, and his ankle bones protruded like big Adam's apples.

Harry was prone to giving up and giving in, his life force not up to the task of running the rat race. It was this rat race that made Harry want to curl up in a corner and die. He just couldn't bear the burden of everyday life, couldn't persevere like most people. Harry was hitting below the curve. His elbows jutted out jaggedly and his breath was reminiscent of stinky socks that had been moldering in a laundry basket for weeks. Harry's complexion was wanting, his sallow skin peppered with volcanic pimples nestled in the stubble of his unshaven face. His eyes were pallid and watery, offsetting his dripping nose above a pair of slightly bluish lips.

Harry hadn't changed his underwear for a couple weeks and still had a week to go before he deemed it necessary. His nails were ragged and fungal and his hands were dominated by repellently swollen knuckles. His demeanor pushed the limits even of motherly love.

Jane Stillwater. Jane had been at the computer for a couple of hours. Her doe-like eyes were reddened by their overlong exposure to the monitor. Jane had man problems. She was simply unable to sustain a relationship that lasted more than a month. She tried to find guys at bars, coffee shops, and even the library, but everyone she dated was a bust. There just weren't any decent men around anymore. Jane was good looking, she had beautiful skin and long legs that seemed to walk on their own. Her hair was expensively coiffed, the locks of which spilled richly onto her shoulders. Jane's inability to find a guy certainly wasn't tied to her physical attributes. It was just that she was, well, picky. She was looking for a soulmate, not some fly-by-night one-night-stand type of guy. So, following a girlfriend's advice, she decided to sign up on CompanionMatch.net in hopes of finding a guy who could make and keep her happy. And here she was, reading and perusing the site for a man. She was hooked, in fact it was just like shopping online. She could look at profiles of guy after guy and not have to deal with the laborious process of finding out what they liked and expected in a woman. It was all laid out for her and she marveled at the convenience of being able to scroll through a bevy of possible matches, each profile piquing her interest with various flavors of hope.

She was tired and about to quit for the night when she came across the profile of Harry Finklestein, God bless him. She loved a good sense of humor and was intrigued to see how this guy had gone over the top in his descriptions of how ridiculously inept he was. Even his profile pictures were ludicrously awful. She marveled at the confidence of a man who would fake a profile in abject jest, she loved this kind of method humor. Her heart swelled with anticipation as she laughed at his profile. Jane had a gut feeling about this guy, a buoyant feeling that bode well with her expectations. Excitedly she clicked on the date button. She had found a perfect match.

Somewhere in the night, Harry stirred restlessly and scratched his groin. Tomorrow was going to be a good day.

A TORPID DISCOURSE

The definition of torpidity is sluggishness. How can one write something enlightening about sluggishness? One answer is to push the pen slowly across the paper, letting the thoughts thicken as they lazily crawl onto the page. The subsequent pool of congealed cogitation may arrive as something brilliant, yet by its delivery remain torpid.

Let's try something else. Step back from the pen and travel up the arm to the mind of a benumbed author. Sooner or later she will write something that could take weeks or even months to complete. This very act of torpidity … would it not construe itself as its own definition regardless of the content?

Perhaps we should take the direct approach and let the words themselves slow down the pace. Words like *bemoan*, *hibernate* and *listless* could shamble across the folio, stumbling over their own letters, their reluctant feet dragging the ink like a smeary ball and chain. A band of lazy adjectives could play the nouns in with a dull lifelessness, their notes heavily spattering the paper like discordant cow flops. Sentences could slowly run on endlessly, reluctant to form themselves into paragraphs, eschewing form and function until they fall off into ellipses … Adverbs could emerge from all-night drinking sessions, their alcoholic stupors already transformed into crusty hangovers that bump into the leaden verbs trudging ahead of them. How about some pointless parentheses (don't even bother to think about these) that drizzle themselves about the page like imitation maple syrup.

Today my friend, a torpid discourse, a lethargic address, an inert speech, unfolds itself onto your lifeless page without even bothering to

WASH

Hitchhikers. Up ahead in the distance. My wiper blades make a slow click-clack as I ponder a decision.

My therapist tells me that I can brighten my future by doing things that I really don't want to do. She calls it "Freedom Training". By doing these things I can expand my horizons a bit; I'm making a conscious decision to open up my life.

I pull my pickup truck over to the side and open the door. I see the couple coming towards me in the rearview mirror. A scraggly pair, male and female, happily make their way to the truck.

"Throw your stuff in the back," I tell them as they come close.

"Okay," they answer simultaneously and sling their packs into the bed of the pickup. The girl slides in first, then the guy. They sit on the bench seat right next to me, two happy faces shiny with rain. My nose twitches involuntarily. A gigantic waft of odor overwhelms me.

It travels into my nose on little piggie feet, sinuously

trotting its way up my nasal cavities straight to my brain where it explodes in a cacophony of patchouli oil, sweat, smoke, and God knows what else.

"Going far?" asks the guy brightly.

"About 20 miles up the road," I reply.

I sense a deeper aroma working its way towards me as it detours first through the upholstery and roof lining of my truck cab. It's a low note redolent with the smell of unwashed skin and dirty feet. It has hair on it, some of it singed, the tiny curled-up balls sticking in my nostrils. The guy and the girl shift around in the seat, making themselves comfortable. I hum an aimless tune as a third layer of stench impolitely announces itself at my nostrils. This smell sits in the middle, right between the other two. It has rounded corners soft at the ends and a soggy squishy middle, kind of like a furry caterpillar that has decomposed on its lonely perch in the forest. The odor has a sharp tang that leaves a distinct aura of selfishness in my invaded brain. It has a scratchiness to it, a restless weasel in rut, its pointy claws digging their way through the delicate softness of my nasal membranes. My brain suddenly combines the three odors into an olfactory parfait and the trinity of stink bowls me over. The stench seems to be mocking me as it weaves its way through my entire body, the sensation a palpable weight bearing down on my very soul.

My eyes start to tear up and with blurry relief I see the turnoff up ahead. I pull over to the side of the road and the couple slides out of the truck, leaving their scent in the cab, a late-night drunk that doesn't want to go home.

"Nice riding with you," says the girl as she leans over to position her face right outside my window.

"Likewise," I say cheerily and wave them goodbye.

The next day I'm sitting in the waiting room at the therapist's office. The door opens and she steps into the room.

"Hello," she says, shaking my hand warmly.

Unwelcome tendrils of her overbearing perfume snake their way into my nostrils. My nose twitches involuntarily again. A gigantic waft of odor overwhelms me.

CHAPTER FOUR

"If Jesus had been hung, we'd all be wearing nooses around our neck."

- Edna

FOUR MOVEMENTS

The young woman sat up straight in her chair, composed herself and blew a purposeful stream of air through the double reed of her oboe. The warm air traveled down a short metal tube into the upper section of the instrument and continued past the keys, entered the lower section and exited through the flared bell.

Eighty-seven other musicians, all dressed spectacularly in their formal performance clothes listened keenly as they tuned their various instruments to the 440 cycles per second of the resultant "A" that hovered smugly in the expectant air of the large concert hall.

Dimitri fidgeted impatiently in his seat. As the concertmaster, he felt it was beneath him to tune with the others so he lingered a little until they were almost finished then entitledly found his pitch.

He was a prodigy, graduating at sixteen from the Juilliard School of Music and finding immediate placement as the first violinist in the Poughkeepsie Symphony Orchestra. For the most part he liked his fellow musicians but strived to maintain a distant relationship with them, not willing to cultivate any intimacy because they were there to support him. Except for the oboist. He had tried to hit on her early on, only to find out that she was consorting with the lowly third violinist who sat directly behind him at the concerts. Awkward.

Dimitri grudgingly rose out of his chair with the other musicians as the conductor walked onto the stage and acknowledged the audience. Then the entire orchestra sat back down respectfully. Dimitri sneered to himself as the conductor importantly tapped his baton against the podium for silence. An eager hush impregnated the air, expectantly waiting for the birth of the first chord and the conductor swept the baton up in a confident upstroke, hesitated slightly, then sliced it down to start the newly discovered Tenth Symphony of Ludwig van Beethoven.

The initial chord blossomed gracefully into the hall, gorgeously voiced by the strings and supported by the woodwinds. The sound started to grow in volume as a solo flute shyly introduced a seven-note theme, each note borne gracefully on the shoulders of the now massive chord. The oboe followed in on tiptoes, joining the flute as Dimitri pictured the pretty young girl playing it, her moist lips wrapped around the shaft of the sturdy mouthpiece, the double reeds of which were stiffened by the pressure of her blow. Her perfectly formed notes intertwined with those of the flute, and the brass section began a slow percussive march underneath, signaling the start of an intrepid musical journey.

The stage was set and Dimitri took a long inhale as he smoothly introduced the counter melody on his eighteenth-century violin. As the gentle strokes of his bow coaxed the violin to issue forth the delicate notes of the second theme, the conductor prepared to bring in the whole orchestra. Dimitri smiled as the maestro slashed his baton downward, briefly unleashing the massive power of the orchestra with a deft movement of his arm, then just as quickly silencing it.

The oboe peeped out of the silent void with a variation of the initial theme, the notes climbing in clever retrograde as they modulated upwards. The entire brass section barged in, and the lone tuba tromped around in the back of the room, creating a jumbled soundscape into which Dimitri's violin began to dance. His instrument weaved its way around the horns and boldly chased the flighty oboe. Dimitri's bow skittered eagerly on the G string and sent its notes fluttering into the air, chromatic butterflies in a hurricane. The percussion section kicked in, forced its way into the storm and tried to take control of the chaos. The conductor swung his baton to and fro in violent arcs, bringing each section into the discordant tumult. Dimitri furiously provoked his violin further into the fray and the instrument responded with sadistic relish as it bullied its way to the top of the crescendo and exploded it into the final chord of the first movement.

The audience sat dumbstruck, the vestiges of reverberation fizzling into the air as the largo of the second movement waited in the wings. The movement started slowly, its namesake tempo defined by the sincerity of the string section minus Dimitri. He sat there listening to the group of strings, yet all he could hear was that damn third violinist behind him, priggishly taunting him with his inferior technique. It was almost as if that bastard knew of Dimitri's desire to make it with the oboist and was deliberately trying to piss him off. Dimitri fumed. He didn't like the way the conductor was handling the tempo. He wanted it even slower so as to make the listeners be disturbed by the primal conflict that was so achingly resounded by the clash of the confused tonal centers.

Dimitri stroked his way into the dissonance, his sonic carriage insistently nudging the dark unpleasantness of the C-sharp minor key into the relative stability of E major. Once established, Dimitri set up a third theme with a gentle ponder in the lower register. As his tone confidently swept through the venue, he fugued with the clarinet and the French horn, each instrument tumbling over one another in an Escheresque loop that begged the questions why and why. The muted orchestra woke up slowly underneath them and revealed itself in a slow yawn that took in the three lead instruments and exhaled them into a harmonic coalescence and subsequent end of the second movement.

The two movements behind him, Dimitri grew impatient, his thoughts leaping over the next section to the challenge of the finale. He discreetly adjusted himself.

The woodwinds were ready to begin the third movement so the conductor politely ushered them into the scherzo. The shy triangle in the back chimed in and embarrassed itself with its limited pitch and timbre. Dimitri ignored it as he spearheaded a jocular interplay with the brass section, each of them dialoguing with frilly abandon and pissing off the English horn who hardly got to play at all, even in the best of times. The music swirled towards its fruition as Dimitri caught a glimpse of the attractive oboist out of the corner of his eye, the seductive promise of her silken thigh peeking out of the long slit of her black dress. Piqued, he brought his attention back to bear on the conclusion of the scherzo, and trilled his way to the close with superior pizzicatos that waggled the smarmy flutes into appreciative submission. The audience stifled an inappropriate urge to clap as Dimitri dismissed the unrequited gesture and forgave Beethoven for his shoddy writing of the third movement.

The finale hovered ahead and Dimitri limbered his hands in anticipation of the fiery histrionics that were to ensue. He started the movement by himself, characteristically ignoring the conductor's ministrations and set a furious tempo with vicious slashings of his bow. The theme be damned, this was beyond the simple conceit of tension and release, no, this was about sex and sweat and longing, the power of which was being revealed by Dimitri's manic instrument. The conductor listened in amazement, his arms uselessly flailing about impotently as the orchestra struggled to keep up with Dimitri's frantic tempo. He was a wild man now, his mouth afroth as he slammed his violin down the scale into the hideously difficult section he referred to as "The Buzz Saw". His fingers became heated by the friction generated from his interaction with the fingerboard as he took the notes from the bottom of the violin and wound them into the screaming intensity of the highest register. The notes seared their way to the ceiling like an upside-down bolt of lightning, which then bounced off and dove into the bassoons, leaving them wounded in their wake and considering early retirement. The notes continued, splintering their way through the percussion section, rendering the kettle drums aghast with envy as they flew by and buried themselves deeply into the ears of the traumatized patrons. Dark incessant notes sprayed out of Dimitri's violin like deadly bullets from a machine gun, mowing down all comers to the melee. The orchestra sheepishly played on, timidly acknowledging Dimitri's prowess as he unabashedly plundered their support for his selfish aggrandizement. Incensed by their struggle to follow him, Dimitri circled his way back around to the players with the theme in tow and extended a sonic olive branch for them to grab onto. The orchestra members gratefully reached out, and, clasping the integrity of the theme, jumped aboard Dimitri's sonic train, settling themselves into cars that whipped behind the chugging violin like a drunken conga line. The music built up to a frightening intensity as the train and the tracks and the entire universe it was in vaporized into a giant whirlwind of sound. Dimitri's soul sang with glee as he spun the miasma around the room with his violin, the sphere increasing in size like a giant snowball as it trundled the audience members with its mass. The ball expanded vertically into a giant column of vibration and as it approached its climax, Dimitri surrendered control to the violent apparition and got sucked into its gravitational thrall. Overwhelmed, the tumescent column erupted with a glorious report, the shockwave of which shook the hall to its very foundations and sent smoldering shards of spent emotion drifting down onto the people in the seats of the deafened auditorium.

They sat there stunned for a while, smothered by a blanket of disbelief until the reluctant aftermath introduced itself to the space left behind by the music and filled it with a shared reverence.

The audience began to clap, slowly at first, fits and starts that gradually gained momentum until the sound turned into an exultant cacophony of approval. The exhausted members of the orchestra collected themselves and, goaded by the conductor, triumphantly stood up as one. The conductor gestured at Dimitri with a show of deference and the audience focused its attention on the young violinist, lauding him with profuse adulations and boisterous respect. Dimitri turned his head and looked back at the orchestra. He was peppered by the congratulations and exaltations of all his colleagues except for the third violinist who had sat down and was pointedly packing his things. Amused, Dimitri turned back to the audience and stood there smiling beneficently. Then the ovation quieted down and stole out of the room, thoughtfully turning off the lights behind it.

The reception was held next door at The Grand, Poughkeepsie's landmark hotel. The large room was appointed lavishly and the wealthy patrons happily milled about, drinking champagne and grazing on musically themed petit fours from the sumptuous buffet. Dimitri strolled about the room, his godlike status cemented by the night's performance. His eyes hungrily swept the large gathering, his focus intent on finding the pretty oboist. He spotted her almost immediately, and his pulse quickened sharply as he noticed she had changed from her black dress to a sexy silver evening gown of which the revealing V cut of the front plunged suggestively towards her nethers.

She was standing across from the pesky third violinist at a small cocktail table and slowly, as if on cue, turned her head and locked eyes with Dimitri. He watched as she dismissed the third violinist and sauntered over. Dimitri pulled her in like a magnet, knowing that no woman had ever been able to resist his talent, his God-given virtuosity and immaculate command of his instrument. She came close to him, her heated desire now unmistakable as she said to him in a voice husky with need, "You were amazing tonight. Call me ... anytime."

Her talented tongue slowly swept her full lips, a harbinger of the warm moisture and sweet sweat to come. She slipped her card into his front pants pocket, lightly grazing his penis then turned around and walked back to her table, her backless dress barely concealing her naked body and the promise within.

Dimitri watched with satisfaction as he spied the dejected slump of the third violinist's shoulders, the poor guy's hopes dashed by the force of Dimitri's dazzling talent. He chuckled disdainfully, picked up the aluminum can on the table, opened his mouth and slammed down his fourth Red Bull as old Beethoven, supposedly laid to rest for the past 194 years, groaned in pain and slowly did a quarter turn in his grave.

TASER HEAD

A wracking cough. A sniffling nose. Bloodshot eyes. Nothing could stop Taser Head.

He got his name way back in '93 when Vinnie shot him with his Taser. Taser Head didn't flinch and Vinnie knew he got him good because there was smoke coming out of his ears. But Taser Head didn't move a muscle — just stood there with his hands in his pockets. *Man, that was cool,* thought Vinnie. Sure, he had lost the bet but it was worth it to see him stand there as 50,000 volts of electricity sizzled through his body.

Vinnie never knew where Taser Head lived, he would just show up out of the blue and hang with him. There was something magical about that man. I mean he was wise, but he never let on, he kept it on the down low. Now flash up to 2021. twenty-eight years later and Taser Head was still slumming around — twenty-eight years, man, that was a lot of living.

Taser Head had done some odd jobs, like working as a fry cook at Vinnie's dad's place back in the day. He had also worked as a janitor at Lincoln High School for a time and drifted in and out of employment in the subsequent years. Probably the strangest job he had done was being the horse sweeper at the annual Veterans' Day Parade, cleaning up after the cops' horses pooped on the road. This was a steady job, unfortunately it only happened once a year. But mostly he had wandered the streets for forty-six years, not paying his taxes and generally keeping to himself.

Taser Head was one funny-looking dude. I mean he was clean and all that, but he always looked a mess. His hair was long and uncombed and his beard was shaggy and unkempt, however he had these amazing blue eyes that could pierce your soul like a love laser to your heart. That's why people hung out with him, plus he would say the darndest things. He had these little stories he would tell, always short, but they would all end with a meaningful twist — a little quirk that would get you thinking about yourself and how you could be a better person. It was weird, man, but it always felt real good to talk to him … real good.

And so He, Taser Head, who in a previous life was known as Jesus Christ, had come again. Only this time he was playing it down — no miracles. After all, he didn't want to get nailed back up on the cross. The last time was a drag.

A SUBLIME CASE OF MISCONCEPTION

The slow drip of time whittled away the present. Large chunks of future lay voluminously on the horizon as the dodo bird wept, its fate predetermined by inevitability. Sarcasm coasted by on a scooter, the rhythmic putt-putt fading in the distance. A martyr walked by, shoes squeaking with turbulence while a large bag of gas whistled softly to itself. Thus the stage was set for the new epoch.

Farley torqued the last bolt on the chromed cylinder head of the 1996 Harley Davidson Softail Fatboy. His sinuously tattooed biceps flexed appropriately as he bore down on the socket wrench. A layer of sweat glistened on his forehead and slowly ran past his eyes, occasionally dripping off his nose. It was hotter than hell in the garage, yet Farley garnered a deep sense of satisfaction from working on his bike. He was almost 6'4" tall and looked like a mean son of a bitch. His unkempt greasy hair touched his shoulders, covering his left hoop earring, the gold of which was tarnished with a long history of tormenting others. His neck had a nasty scar, the result of a clandestine knife fight played out on a sweltering summer's eve in the not-too-distant past. His barrel chest was covered with a leather vest, the back of which bore the insignia of the Poughkeepsie chapter of the Hells Angels Motorcycle Club. The tattoos on his arms and torso consisted mainly of lurid skulls with artistic embellishments, each skull bearing a rictus grin as it tumbled down to the waistband of his black leather pants. A heavy chain was parked on the right side of his belt, its business end securely attached to a set of keys and wallet. His boots were deep black too, accentuated by thick silver buckles that looked like they had kicked the shit out of some unfortunate people who happened to get in Farley's way.

Farley grabbed a shop towel and wiped some of the grease off of his roughly calloused hands. Satisfied, he straddled his bike, twisted the key and fired it up. The garage instantly filled with the sound of thunder as the exhaust bullied its way out of the pipes. He tweaked the throttle and another massive layer of sound obliterated the first as he backed the bike onto the road. With his feet solidly planted, Farley adjusted the bandanna on his head. Then he blew the snot out of his nose and rolled off to the neighborhood center.

It was that special time — the end of the year, when Farley's motorcycle club worked the local Christmas Toys for Tots program. Farley had done his due diligence, helping to solicit funds and buy the toys. Now it was time to wrap them and Farley felt a twinge of anticipatory pleasure as he gunned up to the curb and parked his bike amongst the others. He debarked and walked into the center. He felt at ease as he took in the smell of sweat and leather of his club mates. They greeted him heartily and he returned their warm camaraderie. There was Hipshot, Jonesey, Skull, and Candy Girl — all busy wrapping presents in their motorcycle leathers and cooing to themselves as they gingerly enclosed the gifts. Farley sat down on the bench and with his grease-darkened fingers grabbed a pink Kewpie doll. He let out a sigh of contentment as he started to fold the paper, Christmas music playing softly in the background. And so, truth be told, Farley Davis was in his heart a softie, a big hunk of a pushover. His eyes twinkled merrily as he finished wrapping the doll and reached for another.

HANUKKAH HAM

"Why can't we eat ham, daddy?" asked young Gershom Dershowitz. The smell of bacon from the apartment next door permeated the air, provoking the ire of Gershom's father, Uri.

Uri stroked his long beard and answered , "Son, it's God's will that deems a pig unclean."

He reached over to his Torah and opened it to Leviticus. Pressing his finger to the passage, he read to Gershom, "And the swine, though he divide the hoof, and be cloven footed, yet he cheweth not the cud; he is unclean to you.'"

"Do you understand?" asked Uri.

Gershom nodded his head vigorously, his beautiful *payos* moving accordingly, brown locks of curly hair bouncing in the affirmative. Uri looked at the boy. He was pleased with his development. He felt that his son would mature nicely as a pious Jew, holding the orthodoxy close to the family vest. Uri smiled, then frowned. He could almost hear the bacon sizzling next door, intruding on his thoughts.

Monday, June 23, 2036, was a propitious day for the Putzmann Institute of Genetic Technology. Dr. Jeffery Putzmann was sweating profusely; he had just finished the press conference that marked the most important day of his career. Putzmann did not like being in front of people, particularly the press. He had been grilled and vilified so many times for his controversial research in the field of swine genetics that he loathed public speaking. But this day was different, his project was complete, and he was relieved. He had just introduced the world to its first genetically modified ruminant pig.

He sighed. He had been hired by the pork industry twenty-five years earlier to create a breed of pig that could be certified as kosher. His goal had been to alter a pig's DNA with the metagenomics of a cud-chewing animal. He'd started his bio-processing with goat DNA, rounding the genetic markers and transposing the RNA expression vectors to a breedable solution. In short, he had created a pig that could chew its cud and thus be eligible to fulfill the Torah's requirements for the consumption of meats.

After the announcement of Dr. Putzmann's break-through, the FDA, under pressure from the pork industry, quickly approved the process. A huge breeding infrastructure was set in motion and within six short years the ruminant pig industry had established itself in the mainstream. The price of pork belly futures shot up and the genetically modified pork was finally brought to the table. Simultaneously, the pork industry also worked with a particularly liberal rabbi from the Conservative Jewish community to initiate the religious protocol involved in making ruminant pork meat kosher.

And so it came to pass that on June 23, 2042, exactly six years from the date of Dr. Putzmann's announcement, Naysa Kosher Pork® was introduced to the American public. The liberal Jews, for the most part, were curious. Not a few of them had harbored a secret desire to taste bacon and now the path had been cleared to do so. The Orthodox Jews, on the other hand, were furious. They protested with vehemence, calling the pork an abomination.

The curious among the Jews believed they were aligned with the spirit of the Torah. Yes, it was a loophole, they admitted, but they pointed out that the wearing of wigs by Orthodox Jewish women to cover their hair was also not entirely in line with the intent of the Torah. So, they continued, was the practice of hiring a *Shabbos goy* to do banned labor like turn lights on and off during the Shabbat. The Orthodox Jews fumed but change was inevitable and life went on as usual.

Little Gershom was a man now. He had married, moved out of Brooklyn to Manhattan, and become the father of two healthy boys now aged five and seven. To-day they were excited that Grandpapa Uri was coming over with the entire family to celebrate the last and most important day of Hanukkah with them.

Gershom was extremely nervous because he and his wife Eva were going to break tradition and serve a Naysa Kosher Ham® for the evening supper. The ham was humongous, certainly enough to feed the entire group.

And so it came to pass that the Dershowitz family was gathered together in Gershom's cramped dining room on the last night of Hanukkah. When everybody was ready for dinner, Gershom and Eva gave the gathering a heartfelt blessing, then made an announcement that the night's meal was going to feature a kosher ham. A wave of shock rippled through the group and minor chaos ensued. Finally, Uri's wife Zelda sprang up and shushed everybody. She announced that it was Gershom's right to serve whatever he wanted and to honor and respect the fact that Gershom and Eva had gathered them all there to celebrate Hanukkah.

Assenting murmurs from the group flavored the air and with a little fanfare, Gershom went into the kitchen and brought out the ham. *Oohs* and *ahhhhhsss* followed as Gershom eased the meat onto the table and started to cut it with the carving knife. Uri looked on with disappointment.

"*Oy vey, the boy had such promise,*" thought Uri to himself as he tried to keep an open mind.

A plate was placed in front of him and with great trepidation he cut a small piece of ham and brought it to his lips. Pausing, he glanced at his wife and saw her chewing a bite with enthusiasm. Then he looked around the room and noted that the others were digging into the meal with religious fervor. A sense of discovery fluttered in the air as the smell of the honey-baked ham wafted from Uri's fork to his nose.

Salivating profusely, Uri raised his eyebrows and committed himself to the bite. Instantly a detonation of flavor blasted in his mouth. His eyes rolled upwards as if to seek approval from God. Not seeing anything to the contrary, Uri tucked into the huge piece of pork. He looked around again and saw the entire family still completely engrossed in their meal, the sound of enthusiastic chewing vigorously attendant in the room.

He reflected on his life and concluded that it was a satisfying one. He had raised a good strong family. Zelda had been by his side throughout and had inspired him to try to lighten up. And now it was paying off.

Finished with the meal and very pleased with the taste of the kosher ham, he gave his mouth a final wipe, then put down the greasy napkin. As he did so, he felt a sharp pain in his gut. He got a few more jabs and then heard an ominous rumbling from his stomach. Alarmed and sweating, he stood up and made his way through the cramped room to the small bathroom in the hallway. It was occupied. *Shit.* Sweating even more, Uri pictured the meal he had just eaten. Nagging thoughts trickled in from the back of his mind.

"Did Gershom cook it enough? Have I just contracted trichinosis? Am I going to die?"

He prayed fervently, "Give ear, *Adonai*, to my prayer, heed my plea for mercy. In this time of trouble I call to You, for You will answer me. Please let the bathroom be clear soon. Blessed are You, *Adonai*, Healer of the Sick."

And with this prayer, the bathroom door opened and Zelda sheepishly came out as the sound of the toilet flushing invited Uri in. He shut the door, undid his pants, quickly sat down on the toilet and relieved himself loudly. He instantly felt calmed. He washed his hands and exited the bathroom, leaving the door ajar much to the consternation of the group.

As he sat down, positive thoughts filtered into his consciousness. "Thank You *Adonai*. I'm feeling much, much better. I hope I'm a hundred percent in the morning. And after that, who knows, maybe down the road, I'll try the bacon."

MATING RITUAL

The Golden Bowerbird worked fervently. He had finished making an elaborate structure out of carefully placed twigs. The male bird placed the twigs with great care, for it was the beauty of the bower that would attract the female. In and around the bower, the bird placed a myriad of objects: leaves, feathers, flowers, stones, and shiny materials. Soon a female Bowerbird appeared and the male strutted around the bower, attracting the female even closer. Eventually, after a brief courtship dance, the female acquiesced. The male bird engaged her in an act of copulation.

The deed was done, nature had taken its course.

The male Greater Sage Grouse spied the female grouse in the distance. He began his mating ritual — he flexed his chest and pumped a gallon of air into it thereby causing a great sac to puff out of the upper third of his body. Well within earshot of the female, the male proceeded to rub his wings on the sides of his chest, creating a curious popping sound that attracted the female to him. Fanning his tail feathers, the male grouse shimmied and shook his way to the female, his pops gaining in frequency and intensity. The birds touched briefly, and then they coupled.

The deed was done, nature had taken its course.

The stallion was magnificent. The big and bold horse moved with power and grace, its flowing mane catching the prairie wind. The stallion approached the mare and he pranced and snuffled, then nuzzled and groomed her to elicit a response. The mare wasn't quite ready and she moved away, kicking a little bit, dust puffs coming off her hooves. The male continued to pursue her, his long strides easily keeping pace with the mare. Finally, the mare slowed to a standstill and showed she was ready by deviating her tail from her perineum and urinating copiously, signaling to the male that it was time. The stallion reared up on his powerful legs and covered her back, massively thrusting himself into her.

The deed was done, nature had taken its course.

Wayne was a real player. He piloted his souped-up, chopped-down El Camino down the strip in Las Cruces, New Mexico. He had turned the 550-horsepower beast into a lowrider with custom hydraulics, the kind that popped the car up and down, jinking it like a sprung jack-in-the-box. He pulled up to the light and looked to the car on his left. There were four dolled-up chicas in the car and they started to flirt with Wayne.

He puffed out his chest and, rattling his gold chain, said, "Hey babes, do you want to play?" Then he mashed the hydraulics button into the dashboard and the car lurched into action, sprocketing up and down with sporadic jerks, causing Wayne's head to bob around as he displayed his gold teeth with a sardonic leer.

"Where is the party, man?" said one of the girls to Wayne as he revved his engine.

"Follow me, I'll take you to my club, I can get you girls in for free."

With that, the stop light turned green and Wayne gunned the El Camino down the strip.

Arriving at the club, Wayne escorted the girls inside, and catching a glimpse of himself in the mirror, admired his levitating pompadour. He ran his fingers through it briefly, poofing it up even more, enhancing his ritual display of unbridled machismo. The place was thumping. Big feral tones pushed out of the huge speakers as a DJ pranced about in his exalted cubicle. Wayne ordered drinks and spun around his new friends, culling the one girl in the slinky green dress from the herd.

"Let's dance, girl," he said and bobbed his head around in a gesture designed to convey his willingness to move. The girl let off a little squeal of delight and together they moved out onto the floor. Wayne started pendulating to the primal rhythm, thrusting his pelvis to and fro in an act of simulated sex. They danced and danced and Wayne sweated profusely as he popped and strutted his stuff in front of the girl. Finally, sensing she was ready, Wayne nestled up to her and, mouth almost touching her ear, said, "Let's go to my place." She agreed and they left the club, zooming the El Camino to his apartment.

They entered his crib. Plush shag carpet greeted them as they moved inward. Wayne had decorated the place with shiny objects of art, some hanging on the wall and others perched on pedestals. Wayne put his hands on her from behind and gently nuzzled her neck. Multiple lava lamps in elaborate sconces cast an atmospheric glow on the walls of the room, infusing it with a surfeit of colored light. Wayne eased her toward the bedroom, his eyes dilating and his breathing husky in anticipation of the upcoming union. Still standing, he kissed her again, his thunder stick pressing hard against her war wagon.

"Let's do it," whispered Wayne as he slowly gyrated.

The girl looked into Wayne's eyes and said "Not tonight, chico, I've got a headache."

The deed wasn't done, nature had taken its course.

A SNIFTER OF BODACIOUS CHAGRIN

The mandrill's ass was lit up like a rainbow. I mean someone really went to town on painting the vivid reds and blues all over that thing. And that someone was God, of course, that omnipresent imp with a blatant sense of humor. Forget the doomsday stuff, that's only God working out his frustrations.

I knew God when he was a little kid and was he ever a pain in the ass. He loved to smite things. He would smite all day, riding up and down the block on his yellow Stingray bike. And boy, did he ever cry a lot. The simplest little thing would set him off, like when Mom told him he was grounded after burning down the city with his magnifying glass.

God was slightly dyslexic too. He would read things and get them wrong, then pout when he stood corrected. And that's how he screwed up the Earth. He had gotten the science kit for his thirteenth birthday. The set was huge and the instruction manual was over 800 pages long. God couldn't be bothered with reading the whole thing so he ended up creating life out of carbon-based life forms instead of the requisite boron. This introduced an unstable element to the mix thus causing humans to become self-aware. The botched science project became a real mess and his parents were very mad at him for not paying attention. God tried to fix the problem but the more he tried, the more he screwed it up. Finally, with a snifter of bodacious chagrin, God decided to let sleeping dogs lie and abandoned the project. The earth continued its wacky way around the sun, and God … well, he took off for bigger and better things.

A LITTLE SALIVA NEVER HURT ANYBODY

A dome-shaped glob trembled silently on a blade of clueless grass, its movement exacerbated by the panting of a drooling bulldog. The glob was a former exclamation point that had dropped out of the dog's mouth and dripped into the greenery with a splooshy wobble. Inside the glob, microscopic jellyfish swam in a mucilaginous gel. A wafty cluster of germs slipped off the face of a chunk of ill-defined matter, causing a gray tickle worm to burrow back into the sludge. Five amoebae turned about awkwardly in psyllium-inspired fits and starts as the bulldog continued to pant mercilessly. A penchant unhitched itself from its host and squatted briefly in the turf as another five amoebae slid by discussing the morality of an unrequested hindrance.

An iota of sun hit the glob and caused it to sparkle tenuously. The dog closed its mouth and more globbage spilled onto the grass, slicking it with slime. A child's voice cried out from a convenient distance and the bulldog undid itself from its dribbling repose and ran to its master, a five-year-old girl named Annie. Spying the dog, Annie got down on her hands and knees and waggled her little body, enthusiastically imitating the dog's boisterous arrival. The excited bulldog jumped all over Annie, smothering her face and neck in sloppy kisses, gooey discharges that stuck to her once-pristine face like soggy newspaper.

Suddenly a voice called out from an inconvenient distance. "Annie, Annie," shouted her mom, and her words noodled around the yard for half a titch then found their way into Annie's giggly wet head. Annie started towards the house and she was halfway there when the next set of words hit her.

"It's dinner time, get in here right away, and don't forget to wash your hands!"

Annie slowed and looked down at them. Her hands were fairly clean and Annie was very pleased as she continued towards the house, her face and neck slowly drying in the breeze.

"They're clean, Mom!" shouted Annie as she climbed the steps to the front door.

The dog stayed outside and slobbered on.

THE YAWNER

It started with those pesky reality TV shows. Dennis remembered the first time he got hooked. He was channel surfing late at night when he stumbled across MTV's "The Real World". He was instantly fascinated by the conceit of the over-privileged kids, their insufferable whininess striking a nerve that piqued his curiosity to no end.

Bear in mind, Dennis was not an addictive personality … far from it, he was engaged in life, willfully taking the time to get out in nature to refresh his soul. But this new reality thing was different. It grabbed his psyche, tore it apart, and reassembled it so that he became a bona fide couch potato who voraciously gobbled up the delicious fluorescent pap of the boob tube.

"The Real World" sustained him for a couple of years, then more reality shows began to pop up like humping rabbits multiplying with frantic intensity. Out of the TV dribbled "The Crocodile Hunter", "Emergency Vets", "Making the Band", "American Chopper", "Amish in the City", "Deadliest Catch", "The Real Housewives of Orange County", "Ice Road Truckers", "Jersey Shore", "Duck Dynasty" and "Below Deck".

Each one of these shows sucked Dennis in with cheap charm, the one-dimensional participants making emotional mountains out of inconsequential molehills, indulging their narcissistic upheavals in the irresistible thrall of the camera. Dennis loved it. He stuffed his brain with the tawdry shows, filling his mental gullet with un-adulterated crap, watching show after show until his eyes turned red and twitched spasmodically.

Then the yawns came. They started around the sixth year of his electronic addiction. They came randomly at first, nothing to be alarmed about, just a few good yawns here and there but curiously, he didn't feel tired.

Slowly he began to notice them more and more, es-pecially during the time he watched his reality TV shows. He started to get the feeling that these shows were the cause of his yawning, yet he was powerless to stop watch-ing. The shows dug into his soul and scooped out the last vestiges of natural thought that stubbornly remained, leaving his mental countenance as desolate as the surface of the moon. By yawning, his body was telling him that he'd seen enough. And still he couldn't stop watching the TV.

The yawns began to affect his everyday life, coming

to him involuntarily as he went about the day. He yawned at breakfast, yawned on the bus, yawned at the bank, yawned while he was going to the bathroom, yawning and yawning until his jaws became stiff and sore. He cracked down on his TV watching and began to wean himself off the electronic nipple, each day paring a few minutes from his visual consumption until he was finally able to stop. Unfortunately, his body had permanently changed and the yawns persisted.

People began misinterpreting his behavior, thinking he was simply bored at what they had to offer. He just could not stop, even yawning as he made love to his girl-friend. She was disappointed with his behavior, thinking incorrectly that he was bored with her, and subsequently ended their relationship.

His diet suffered greatly, going from slow-cooked meals to instant TV food of the just-add-water, mi-crowave and eat-out-of-the bag variety. His physiology changed, turning his once strong muscles to globulating fat and souring his sweat, creating an unpleasant odor that overwhelmed anyone unfortunate enough to be in his proximity. Things had gone so far downhill that he couldn't hold onto his job, his boss unwilling to pay somebody who seemed uncaring about work.

Jobless, he dipped into his meager savings and swift-ly spent them down until he could no longer afford his rent. In time the landlord came to his apartment and issued Dennis an eviction notice. He was taken aback by Dennis' apparent indifference, not realizing that Dennis was engaged in an involuntary reflex. Dennis was cast adrift, his homelessness being the straw that broke him down. He got no sympathy from strangers — they didn't want to have anything to do with the disheveled smelly guy who couldn't be bothered to care enough about their help to stop yawning.

Unprepared for this situation, Dennis became increasingly fragile and finally collapsed in the street, kneeling to the pavement, his splintered soul spilling out of his eyes, the very instruments that led to his downfall.

And thus began his nascent acting career as a break-out TV star in a new show about people with unusual afflictions, a soon-to-be hit reality series called "Life is a Bitch".

THE ENDLESS END

The third dimension of a dot is a line. It's just that you happen to be looking at the line head-on. The fourth dimension of a dot is its placement in the now, fronted and backed by the past and the future. And that line of the dot is an infinite quantity piercing the unknown with its unrelenting presence, the infallible structure of being.

Damien's time was almost up. His body lay in the bed clinging to life, like the delicate parchment of dried birch bark barely on the tree, softly working its way free in the gentle breeze. His breathing was labored, the newly present death rattle alarmingly loud like the sound of a steel marble being shaken in an aerosol can. This was all part of the natural process of death which was now enfolding Damien's vitality with a quiet smother. His heart, once strong and courageous, now settled into a resigned rhythm, its obligation to beat resolving towards an inevitable conclusion. That heart, being not only the instrument of physical life, but also the gateway to the true spiritual awakening of the beyond.

And so it is this moment, this inscrutable moment, that turns out to be merely a cross-section of the never-ending end that continues forever and before, the blip of which Damien is just a dot.

MORNING GLOW

Ernie had never experienced a morning like this. He had watched the sun tentatively peek its head over the horizon and then, gathering strength, hoist itself up to its current morning position. The clouds scudded along on a fresh breeze, little pufflets scouring the sky to a salubrious blue. The birds sang mightily as they hopped back and forth from the telephone line to the power wire, their wings half flapping as they performed their myriad mating rituals. A rich earthy tang permeated the air as the sun's warm rays snuggled their way into Ernie's jacket.

He had been walking for hours now, aimlessly strolling the recently dewed grass of the pasture. The sun bestowed its magnificence on the land. The bluish stones by the burbling brook warmed up steadily as the big brown cows lowed their approval downstream. A dragonfly buzzed nearby, its four gossamer wings vibrating in a cheery hum. A huge oak tree stood stolidly among the ranks of white birch, their unique barks glowing with health as they soaked up the light. A weathered wooden fence zig-zagged its way up a lumpy hill, occasionally stopping for a big boulder, then resuming its way upward. Chubby green caterpillars inched their way among the unpretentious dandelions.

Ernie contentedly strode amongst them. And the sun, oh the glorious sun, continued its way upwards, conducting this symphony of life ever forward. A tiny ant crawled amidst magnificent mushrooms, maneuvering its way around rich loamy chunks of soil. Winding down a dirt road, the sounds of a distant barnyard soughed their way to Ernie's ears with the gentle touch of a silken kiss.

Suddenly, Ernie heard a squishy sploosh. He grimaced as he looked down and saw that he had stepped in a huge pile of cow shit. The smell hit him in the face like a rancid old mop, and he thought to himself, "So much for the beautiful day."

Ernie slowly turned around and hobbled his way back home.

THE UNSTORY

I can't write anymore. The well has gone dry, my pen no longer serves me. My mind is a blank slate, the writing chalk broken into crumbles, cremated remains of an old crone.

I crack my knuckles, making a dull popping sound that is too anatomical, too real. I look at my coffee cup, its cold emptiness aligned with my blankness and wonder if I will ever write again. A thin prickling sensation snakes its way from the bottom of my spine to my shoulders. My resistance feeds the feeling and it starts to snowball into panic as it makes its way to my forehead. My goddamn forehead wrinkles tightly, the panic now a spring wound up to maximum capacity, its pressure building up inexorably.

A bird coos softly outside, its soothing sounds completely lost in the deafness of my fear. I want to cry out to God, "Please, please give me something to write about," but God doesn't listen to me anymore.

The fear of my unfulfilled destiny propels me into

the kitchen and I peruse the contents of the refrigerator, aimlessly searching for something to eat, something to fill the gaping void in my heart where creativity once lived. The loss is palpable and as I eat the cold leftover garlic bread my mind despairs. A car alarm goes off in the street, its changing cacophony greeting my anxiety with a jangling overture, a knife piercing my brain. I cry. It starts to rain and it seems like the world is crying with me, weeping infinite tears of sadness through the saturated atmosphere.

Hours pass and the milky sun disappears, diminished by the dusk of the early evening. It's 7:30 p.m. and I head upstairs to my bedroom, each creak of the old stairs coming to my ears with wooden melancholy. I lay myself down on top of the soft bed and close my eyes. I pray that I'll be able to write something tomorrow. The long night looms ahead. As I drift off to sleep, caught between two worlds, my muse shows up and gently tucks me in.

"Good night and sweet dreams," she says, "I'll see you in the morning."

A DISTANT BELL

You could barely hear the church bell off in the distance, five stalwart clangs making their way doggedly to the ears of the tired workers. The truck shut down, its clattering suddenly mute as the unrelenting sun shone on the parched field, all business and no play. The scorching heat withered the air in dry silence as a cricket stubbornly chirped the temperature, each degree ticked off with reluctant determination.

Ruíz gripped the handle of his *coa de jima* loosely as he finished cutting the agave leaves and winnowed the tool into the center of the cactus. With a deft flick of the sharp instrument, he severed the heart from the plant, leaving it on the ground in a row of others to be picked up by the truck.

He'd been working all day, stopping every so often to take huge gasping gulps of water from his plastic gallon jug. The jug was filthy with the dust of three months of hard work in the field, each day a monotonous slog of backbreaking labor. The ringing bell coincided with quitting time, so Ruíz plodded over to the truck and climbed into the back, his feet seeking the solid bed underneath the assorted agave hearts. The agave was headed from the highlands of Los Altos to the town of Juarez where it would be processed into Casa Campana tequila. It was a boutique operation, the small batches brewed and fermented by masterful artisans steeped in the craft of distillery.

Ruíz could care less. He was simply going back to the dormitory where he would mutely share his tribulations with the other dusty men. Even amidst the solidarity of his compatriots, he felt desolate and alone, motivated solely by the need to make money to support his family.

After arriving at the dormitory Ruíz went to his room and eased himself down on the bed. He lay there until he heard the distant tolls of the church bell, seven of them. He got up and walked to the kitchen. It was time for dinner and he prepared his beans on the dilapidated stove. Every night Ruíz ate the same thing, he had little energy left from his hard day's labor to cook anything else. He was a dry sponge, empty and stiff, just waiting for something in his life to fill him up again, making him moist and pliable and bright with renewed purpose.

After nine tolls of the bell drifted over from the village, Ruíz put himself to bed and slept the dreamless blue sleep of exhaustion, his breath a soft snore in the hushed night. Five AM came quickly as Ruíz rose with the others, all of them stretching and yawning together as they rubbed the sleep out of their eyes.

After breakfast, he crowded into the back of the truck with the men. The truck spluttered to life and lurched onto the dirt road, making its way to the field, noxious black smoke spilling out of the rusty muffler. Today was Saturday, the last day of the six-day work week, and Sunday was around the corner, coming none too soon. His day of rest. He anticipated the comforting sound of the church bell calling him to the cool pews within. Sunday was his day to relax, to step off the treadmill of obligation and reconnect with his Lord and Savior Jesus Christ. For it was through Jesus that Ruíz felt the solace and purpose in life and it was through the church that he felt a sense of belonging. Stripped of his family, these were the only things he lived for.

Sunday finally came and so did the bell, holy and small in the distance. Ruíz donned his nice clothes and made a cold breakfast. He ate it slowly, chewing quietly as he thought about his beloved family. Presently he walked out the door into the brilliant, scorching day. A mass of monarch butterflies rose in front of him, filtering the surrounding sunlight with their sheer numbers. There were so many of them he could feel the movement of air from their wings, small breaths combining to wrap him into the sighing gentleness of the warm air. The solitary cloud expanded slowly out of the blue sky as more butterflies surrounded him, smothering him in a living cocoon of bright color. He breathed shallowly, fearful of accidentally inhaling one of the fluttering insects. They clung to his arms, his legs, his neck, his torso, they were everywhere, trembling on his body with a tenacious grip. He began to struggle a little and as he did a mixture of fear and joy welled up in his chest, suffocating him with raw emotion. He felt tears running down his cheeks, warm tracers of cry coming out of his eyes like molten silver and down his face and neck amongst the butterflies, soaking into the clean white cotton of his shirt. The butterflies kept landing on him, packing every little space with their delicate bodies, turning him into a colorful apparition on this bright day, this shiny random moment in Ruíz's life where something unexpected and uncalled for was happening to him. Overwhelmed with feeling, Ruíz sat down on the dusty ground, the butterflies shifting to accommodate his movement. He looked up at the sky and his mind focused on one thought, the thought that everything that happened to him, no … that happened to everyone, yes … everything that happened to everything was always a coincidence. The butterflies, the beans, the sun, the agave hearts, the church, the truck, all these things happened just at the right time, just at the right place. Just so. Everything.

Ruíz closed his eyes in the wonder of his epiphany and right then, just at the right moment in time, in a perfect coincidence, the distant bell started ringing again, calling him gracefully to the church.

EPILOGUE

This page unintentionally left blank.

PREFACE

My first foray into the dynamic world of flash fiction began eight years before the outbreak of the twitterverse. Now, I'm excited that my penchant for writing tiny stories has become appropriate for the attention challenged masses of the First World.

I'm a lucky guy because, like you, I was able to overcome the seemingly impossible odds of being born, and I appreciate my ability to shoehorn a bunch of prose into a tight loafer for your reading pleasure.

So, my cherished reader, it is my impassioned wish that you be entertained by the following words as much as I have enjoyed writing them.

Cheers!
Tony LeHoven
5/9/22